ALWAYS YOUR LOVE

A GOTHIC REGENCY ROMANCE

ELLIE ST. CLAIR

Facebook: Ellie St. Clair

Cover by AJF Designs

Do you love historical romance? Receive access to a free ebook, as well as exclusive content such as giveaways, contests, freebies and advance notice of pre-orders through my mailing list!

Sign up here!

Also By Ellie St. Clair

Standalones

Always Your Love
The Stormswept Stowaway
A Touch of Temptation
Unmasking a Duke

For a full list of all of Ellie's books, please see
www.elliestclair.com/books.

1

Hannah Blackburn needed a moment.

A moment alone. A moment away from the crush of people. A moment away from Byron.

She took a shaky breath, closing her eyes as she pressed her hand against her throat and leaned against the back of the door.

As she began to restore her equilibrium, she opened her eyes, and allowed her gaze to wander over the shadows among the bookshelves, created by the dwindling flame in the fireplace at the far end of the room. It seemed she had stumbled upon a library. It had been the first door she had tried. The room was so full it was near bursting, with not only the expected books but also statues, vases, portraits, and unused frames littering the space.

A chesterfield sat in front of the fire, and Hannah took a step forward, drawn toward the warmth and comfort.

"What are you doing in here?"

Hannah jumped, whirling around to determine the voice's origin. Her heart pounded within her chest, but she was proud she hadn't emitted even the slightest of sounds.

"Who's there?" she demanded, though there was a break in her tone.

"Did I frighten you?" His voice was dry, containing a hint of sarcasm, although Hannah didn't see what could possibly be amusing about his words.

"You startled me," she said, peering into the shadows, finally making out his silhouette in the corner, sitting in an armchair that had been pushed back against the wall. "I'm sorry to have disturbed you," she said, thrown slightly off balance by the stranger who didn't seem to have any desire to make his identity known. "I'll leave you now."

"Don't go." The command he issued somehow contained a hint of pleading in it, as though he was desperate for company. While she knew she should leave, Hannah found herself rooted to the floor, curious to solve this mystery of a man.

"Tell me why you've escaped the festivities," he continued.

Hannah wandered over to the chesterfield now, where she would be closer to the enigma's corner of solitude.

"I don't particularly enjoy parties," she admitted, though why she was saying so to a stranger she couldn't even see, she wasn't sure. Perhaps it was because, with his visage obscured, he was unthreatening. "I find I can best get through them if I take a minute to myself now and again."

"I see," he said, and she felt that, more than simply offering platitudes, he actually did understand. "Are you certain you should be alone, unchaperoned?"

"Likely not," she said, looking down at her hands. "But my mother would not be particularly pleased to accompany me away from the party."

"You're to show yourself off – find a husband then?" His

voice was deep and rough, as though it had been hindered by disuse.

"Something like that," she said softly.

"Well, you certainly won't find one in here," he said, a slight bit of rueful laughter accompanying his words, and Hannah wondered what it was about him that caused him to discount himself from fulfilling such a role.

"Are you married?" she asked, her curiosity getting the better of her.

"No."

"You have no wish to be?"

There was a long pause.

"No."

"Well," she said, needing to fill the silence suddenly, as the air that had previously carried some comfort in it suddenly became tense at his terse replies. "Not to worry. It seems I have already found myself one."

"Oh?"

"It's actually the purpose of this party tonight – to celebrate our betrothal. I don't know him particularly well. Our parents have arranged it all, you see. It's odd, isn't it? That I am to spend the rest of my life with someone I hardly know?"

He was silent for a moment once more, and Hannah longed to walk over and see what this man looked like. It was both disconcerting and yet at the same time freeing to speak to someone practically invisible.

"Are you sure he would make you a good husband?" the stranger finally asked, and Hannah sensed that there was more behind the words than a simple question.

"I don't know," she said, for he echoed the very sentiment she worried about. "It doesn't seem to matter."

"It should," he said, surprising her by standing. He

walked around the perimeter of the room, never stepping into the dim glow from the fire. The room held no other source of light – the wall sconces, candles, or lanterns were all dark. "Do not give your life away to someone who doesn't deserve it."

Hannah stood, taking a few steps toward where he had paused in the corner of two bookshelves. He was tall, she could ascertain from his silhouette, his build lean and seemingly strong. His hair nearly brushed his shoulders, quite opposed to the style of the day. Her fingers itched to paint the scene before her.

"You seem to know more than you are saying," she said, knowing she should leave the room and not question her marriage, for it was too late. The betrothal had been announced, and there was no going back now. Her parents would never allow it. "Tell me what I should be aware of – please?"

He hesitated, and she could sense that he was trying to decide whether or not to share what she now so desperately needed to know.

"Your soon-to-be husband can be a brute, Lady Hannah," he said, and she gasped when he said her name, though why wouldn't he know who she was? He was at her betrothal party, after all, even if he was hiding away in the library. "He will not be true to you, will give you nothing but pain. Why do you think they are marrying him off to a woman like you? Should not a future earl be doing much better for himself? Your parents must be desperate."

Hannah could not have been more shocked had he slapped her in the face. She couldn't deny, however, that his words held truth to them, and caused the tingles of unease that had accompanied her the few times she had been with her betrothed to turn into full tremors.

"Pardon me, but who are you to say such things to me?" she finally managed, and his chuckle was low and humorless as he stepped forward, staying just beyond the soft light.

"I am a man who tells the truth, for I have no reason to pretend, like the rest of them out there, cloaked in their fineries and their lies, obscuring their horrible souls beneath. With me, it is as you see it."

"And yet you hide in the shadows," she challenged, angry now that he would throw out such accusations without revealing anything about himself.

"You are correct," he acknowledged. "It is where I belong."

EDMUND WONDERED why the girl was still here. He had to give her some credit – most young women would likely have gone running the moment they found themselves alone in the library with him. Although she hadn't yet actually *seen* him. The moment she did, he knew she would flee, as did everyone else with the unfortunate chance to see his visage. It was why he never should have come, why he belonged hidden away at the remote estate his father had been more than happy to give him, especially when he had promised to remain there.

Edmund would have preferred to not be here tonight, but his mother had insisted he attend. She felt the whole family should be supporting this marriage. Perhaps she knew they must do all within their power to force it ahead.

What was left of his heart went out to the girl before him. She was short and slim, with wide brown eyes and a waif-like quality about her. He had hoped that the woman his brother was to wed would be strong enough to hold her own against him. But this woman? She would likely break before him. He did admit, however, that she had some backbone, to remain here talking to a stranger in the darkness, especially after his insult.

He didn't overly care about the consequences that came with warning her away from his brother and what awaited her were she to continue on with this marriage.

"It's not too late," he said, fighting the strange desire that coursed through him to step closer to her and touch the soft skin of her cheek where the firelight flickered. "You can go, still."

For a second, he wasn't sure if he was warning her away from him, or from his brother. Then he realized it didn't matter. It would be best for her if she ran away from his entire sordid family.

"I can't," she said, shaking her head with some melancholy. "It's been decided. My parents would never allow me to cry off now."

"Tell me," he said, the need to know coming from deep within him, "have you ever known a man before?"

"Have I ever... Oh! Of course not!" she exclaimed, her eyes widening as she peered at him, attempting to make him out in the darkness. "How could you ask such a thing?"

He shrugged, even though he knew she couldn't see him. "I was not trying to imply anything untoward. I was simply wondering if you have ever known any tenderness, so that you will have a fond memory to look back upon once your husband comes to you."

She audibly swallowed.

"No," she said, her voice just above a whisper. "I have never even been kissed."

He reached out, unsure what caused him to do so, and

took her hands in his before gently pulling her toward him to join him in the shadows. He should now place his hands on her shoulders, turn her around, and steer her out the door. Away from him, from his darkness, from all the base instincts that drove him.

But he didn't. While his dark heart hadn't shown compassion to another person for years now, he felt an unnatural need to protect this woman, to provide her with all he knew his brother never would.

He didn't know why she went along willingly, unresisting. But comply she did, stepping forward, joining him in the darkness, tilting her head back to look up at him, and searching out his face.

Fortunately, however, the light was too dim and the fire too small for them to distinguish anything but silhouettes of one another.

It was enough for him to know where she stood, and he reached out slowly so as not to scare her, before he finally allowed his fingertips to graze the soft, smooth skin that had called to him since she had entered the room. He began to tilt his head down toward her, giving her every opportunity to back away, to run, to go tell all of the others about the monster in the library.

But she didn't. She stood there, expectant, head tilted back, the only sign of a change in emotions the increased speed of her breath, which puffed against his lips.

Until finally, his lips reached hers. He grazed them upon hers, softly tasting, testing, tempting her. When she stood on her tiptoes, placed her hands upon his chest, and leaned into it, he was lost.

He moved his lips over hers, still gentle, but now exploring, caressing, providing her with all of the care she deserved in a first kiss. He slid his hands down her face, her neck, her shoulders, until they wrapped around her back and pulled her against him.

She had been telling the truth of her inexperience, and yet it was her enthusiastic response that fueled him, driving him to delve deeper, to taste her sweet innocence. It flowed through him powerfully, reminding him that he was the last man who should be touching her. His brother might treat her ill, but at least she likely wouldn't be disgusted when she stared upon his face.

It was that thought that was finally strong enough to make him pull back, to leave the sweetness of her lips, though it was a moment before he could step away from her.

"There," he said gruffly, though inwardly he cursed, "remember that."

She stepped back from him, leaving him feeling bereft at the loss of her closeness. He didn't know how long they stood like that, staring at one another, suspended in indecision, until a shriek from beyond the room captured their attention.

"I must go," she said, and then, turning in a swirl of fabric and the scent of lavender, she was gone.

2

Hannah's heart hammered against her ribs as she left the library and all of its secrets and hurried down the corridor. A cluster of people surrounded the doorway to one of the other sitting rooms, which surprised her – should they not all be in the drawing room and the space which had been fashioned into a ballroom for the night?

The crush of people crowded around the entryway were now murmuring among themselves. Hannah weaved around the onlookers, coming to a halt when she saw Lady Heatherstone lying in its entrance, while another woman attempted to revive her with smelling salts and a maid ran off for additional help. Hannah lifted her hand to cover her mouth, wondering what could have caused the woman to faint away, when movement within the room caught her eye and she looked up.

The scene in front of her caused her to freeze completely.

For there was Lord Byron Marshville – her betrothed – fastening his trousers.

In front of him was a young woman Hannah knew only by name, hastily shoving pins into her hair.

Hannah couldn't even identify any of the emotions that rushed through her, so stunned she was – by the sight before her and, if she were being honest, by all that had occurred between her and the stranger within the library. What a turn of events this all was, she mused. The difference between the two simultaneous occurrences? She had not been caught – and what happened here seemed to have gone far beyond a kiss.

She would have thought the woman in front of her would be embarrassed at being found so compromised, but it seemed the opposite was true. A smug smile lined her face, particularly when she found Hannah standing there.

The satisfaction in her eyes flickered, however, when she looked just over Hannah's shoulder.

"What is the meaning— my God. Byron." Lord Heatherstone had joined the group in the doorway, stepping over his wife to enter as he took in the scene. "Close this door immediately!" he bellowed, before pointing his finger at his son, his expression furious. "You," he said, nearly sputtering, "into my study. Now. This betrothal party is over."

Hannah took a step backward as the door closed in front of her, suddenly becoming an observer despite the fact that her future was indelibly intertwined with what had just occurred. Her fiancé had just compromised another young woman in front of half the *ton*.

Somehow, she doubted she would soon be a bride. And all that she felt at the thought was relief.

EDMUND HADN'T FOLLOWED Lady Hannah into the hall to determine the source of the hysterics. In truth, he hadn't been overly interested. He guessed some fool had cuckolded another, or two women had appeared wearing the same gown. He didn't overly care. All that mattered to him was the end of this blasted party and his return to Hollingswood Manor, which he had called home for five years now.

Five years, since his previous life had ended and his new one had begun. A life that had no room for kisses with beautiful young women with too-wide eyes who reached deep within his black soul and stirred a heart that hadn't beat for any reason beyond keeping his blood flowing through his veins for a long time now.

He was surprised, then, by the smattering of footsteps outside the doorway, followed by blessed silence. That is, until he heard his father start bellowing. There was an answering yell, and finally even Edmund was curious.

He walked over to the door, opening it a crack so that he could better hear.

"Your son *will* marry my daughter!" roared an indignant, portly man as he walked backward down the corridor, one hand in the air, a finger pointed toward Edmund's father. Beside him walked a pretty young woman, with what Edmund assumed was her father's jacket wrapped tightly around her. "Or I will see you as ruined as she now is!"

Finally, they were gone, and Edmund opened the door wide enough to step out into the hallway, looking down to see his father pushing his brother into his study.

Edmund decided he best simply avoid the entire sordid affair, but his father unfortunately caught sight of him.

"Edmund!" he called out. "Come here."

"Thank you, Father, but I'm off to bed," he responded, but his father would have none of it.

"My study, Edmund," he said, his face hardened into a mask that even Edmund had difficulty ignoring, "now."

Edmund sighed and, despite every cell in his body telling him to do otherwise, he strolled lazily down the hallway, just to provoke his father.

Fortunately, upon his arrival in the study, he found that he was not the object of his father's chagrin – how could he be, when he had remained hidden in the library all night?

His father, Lord Heatherstone to everyone else, was pacing the study floor, his hands behind his back. Every now and then he looked up at his first son, Byron, who stood by the fireplace, one elbow upon the mantel as he stared his father down with nonchalance.

"I really don't see issue, Father," Byron said casually as Edmond entered, taking a seat in the corner. "It was a simple tryst, that's all. It means nothing."

"A simple tryst in front of half the *ton*! How could you be so stupid? You have ruined her," his father bit out. "How am I supposed to show my face in society now? Her father is a marquess!"

"And you're an earl," Byron said, shrugging. "Hardly a difference."

"Hardly a difference, you say," Lord Heatherstone muttered. "You're a fool, Byron."

"A fool and your heir," he said. "Besides, I am already engaged. Do you not recall the entire purpose of tonight's party?"

"One *you* apparently forgot," his father huffed, his pacing resuming across the navy Aubusson that covered the middle of the room. He looked up at the portrait of his father, Edmund's grandfather, that hung above the desk as though seeking his advice. The portrait stared down in disapproval and Edmund shuddered. He preferred to avoid reminders of his grandfather. "You've ruined one woman, yet we need you to marry the other."

"Why?" Edmund asked, the first thing he had said since entering the room.

His father shot him a look of disdain. "Had you paid any attention to this family's affairs, you would know, Edmund," he said, though the question did cause him to stop pacing. "We need Lord Exner's money."

"Ah, so the young woman has a significant dowry, then."

"She does," his father confirmed. "We've had some... losses lately." He looked over at Byron, who didn't show any remorse, his lips twisted in a wicked smile. Edmund was aware that some of that money had gone to paying off the families of women who were not particularly pleased with where Byron's affections had led. "Unfortunately, there were too many witnesses tonight to buy their silence." He looked at his eldest son. "Why now, Byron, why here?"

Byron shrugged again. "Melody enjoys my... taste of seduction," he said, his lips turning in remembrance, causing his father to nearly choke.

After a few minutes of silence, Lord Heatherstone sighed, running a hand through his hair. "If only you hadn't chosen your mother's sitting room," he said, shaking his head. "Lord knows she will never be able to remove such an image from her mind." He took a deep breath. "You will have to marry the chit, Byron, though in your actions, you have likely ruined both this woman and your betrothed, though you don't seem to overly care. I had the fathers of both women nearing apoplexy as they left, determined that each would marry you."

If only they knew the truth – then they would be running from the family.

Lord Heatherstone finally took a seat behind his desk,

drumming his knuckles on the table, once, twice... until they stopped. His head tilted as though an idea had come to him, and he slowly turned his head until he had Edmund in his sights.

"Or..." he murmured, and Edmund began shaking his head, not wanting anything to do with this entire affair. "We could marry the Exner girl to *you*."

"Absolutely not," Edmund said, standing. His blood began to stir at the thought of Lady Hannah, but he refused to entertain the idea that she could be his, for he was smarter than that. "Besides, she would never have me."

"She would have no choice," his father argued. "That, or be ruined. What other man is going to offer for goods that weren't enough for your brother? Her father is desperate to have her married off – there was some scandal with her sister and this girl is already four-and-twenty."

Edmund found that difficult to believe. He had thought her to be twenty at the very oldest.

"Yes," Lord Heatherstone said with a smile, warming to the idea now. "This will work perfectly. I will speak with the fathers of both women tomorrow."

"I'll not marry her," Edmund insisted, but his father appeared not to be listening. Edmund persisted. "Her father won't agree to it. Not when he sees me. Or knows where I live."

His father waved a hand in the air. "Hollingswood can be improved. Add a few servants, some new furniture, some wallpaper, good as new."

He looked Edmund up and down, but said nothing. No words were needed. For they all knew the truth – the estate could be improved but there was no hope for Edmund. He was who he was, and nothing could change it.

"And if I refuse?" Edmund asked, arching his eyebrow.

"Then I shall sell Hollingswood," his father said, narrowing his eyes. "I will need the money in lieu of what the girl's dowry will bring our family. You will have to return to London."

"You wouldn't," Edmund said, not believing his father. He was as happy about Edmund's omission from society as much as Edmund himself was.

"Test me," his father said, biting out the words, and Edmund finally had to reluctantly admit defeat.

For he would never return to Society. He would die first.

"I SHALL MARRY *WHOM*?"

"Lord Edmund – Lord Marshville's brother."

Hannah stared at her father in shock over dinner the following evening. Her mother was silent at the other end of the table, her head bent low over her plate.

"But... I've never met the man."

She hadn't. She had heard rumors about him of course. Everyone had. Lord Edmund had been injured in the war, barely surviving. He was, apparently, now so scarred that he was unrecognizable. He hid away in one of the family estates far from London, and hardly ever returned, except to visit his mother now and again.

She thought of last night's stranger. The truth was, she could hardly think of anything else but the man, and the press of his lips upon hers. While it was true it had been her first kiss, she could hardly imagine that there could be any better. She only wished that she knew who he was, what his name was. He had seemed bitter, yes, but she had sensed that there was goodness within him, that he had felt sorry for her and her entire situation.

If only…

But it didn't seem to matter what she wanted anyway. Even if she did know his identity, she was apparently bound to marry one of Lord Heatherstone's sons. No one seemed to care which one it was.

"I'm sure he will make you a fine husband," her father said, but even he couldn't mask his own disbelief in the words. "Just have to give it a chance, is all."

"Why are you so determined to marry me off?" she asked, imploring him, looking from her mother to her father. Her father set his jaw determinately, but something in her gaze must have softened him, for he finally sighed and relented.

"You know why. Justine all but ruined your chances of ever marrying with the scandal she caused."

Scandal was an understated description for when her sister had run away with one of the footmen to be married in Scotland. One her mother had never quite recovered from, and that her father still had not forgiven her for.

"We want to ensure that you marry well, into a family that can look after you. You have no brothers, Hannah, and we do not know how well your cousin Anderson will look after you one day."

Hannah sighed, wishing she could look after herself, but what her father said was true. If only she was the sister who had enough backbone to run away with a man of her choosing, who wasn't the good girl always doing as her parents bid. But she couldn't help it. She had always been that way.

"Lord Heatherstone and his son will secure a special license. Apparently, he is eager to return to his estate in Cheshire and has agreed to marry you only if you can return as soon as possible."

"What?" Her fork fell to her plate with a clatter. "But I wasn't to be married for months!"

Her father shook his head. "I'm sorry, Hannah. The truth is, we don't want to see you go so quickly either. But I'm sure you will be back to visit often."

Again, lies, Hannah realized, anger beginning to burn in her belly. If all was to be believed, Lord Edmund would have no desire to return to London. He would keep her hidden away in Cheshire. Turmoil began anew within her. If the stranger's words about Lord Byron Marshville had been true, then what would his brother be like?

"Mother?" she implored, but when her mother finally looked up, it was with tears in her eyes before she lifted her glass and drank its entire contents.

"We best prepare your trousseau," was all she finally said, as Hannah's stomach sank.

There was no going back now.

3

Why was the parlor so dimly lit? Hannah wondered as she arrived at the Heatherstones' townhouse with her parents. She had been given three days to prepare. She would be married by special license this morning and then would be off to Hollingswood Manor near Cheshire, a carriage ride that would take two days. She would be going alone with her husband but for her maid, who seemed to carry as much trepidation about the future as Hannah herself did.

They were greeted by Lord and Lady Heatherstone, who didn't exactly look as though they had completely recovered from the affairs at the party. The only one who seemed unaffected was Lord Byron Marshville himself, who remained seated in a carved Louis XV chair in the drawing room, waving a jaunty hello when they walked in.

Hannah nodded, looking around for the man she was going to spend the rest of her life with.

"Where is Lord Edmund?" her father demanded, apparently thinking the same thing.

"He shall be with us momentarily," Lord Heatherstone said, looking nearly as ill as Hannah felt.

There was a sound from behind them, and they all turned as one when a figure filled the doorway. As he stepped through the threshold, Hannah had to place a hand over her mouth to cover her gasp.

He was tall, as were the rest of the men in his family. His long, dark hair was pulled back in a queue reminiscent of days of old. But it was his face that had captured her attention – how could it not? One side was near perfection, all chiseled jaw and cheekbone, a fine eyebrow over a blue eye that pierced right into her. It was the other side though, that no one would ever be able to ignore. It was... well, it was destroyed. The top part was a mangle of scars, the eyebrow gone, the skin stretched over his eye so low that it appeared nearly closed. The scars continued down his face to the side of his nose, where they began to return to the skin he had been born with.

He faced them all down with a challenging expression, as though he was waiting for them to swoon or to scream or, most likely, to call the marriage off. Hannah heard her mother let out a bit of a whimper, while her father began looking between Lord Edmund and Hannah as though he was second-guessing handing over his daughter.

"Well," Lord Heatherstone said, clapping his hands together, discomfort covering his face. "Shall we get on with it?"

There was more behind his question than a simple statement to move along the wedding. In truth, he was obviously asking if Hannah and her family were still willing to go through with it after seeing Lord Edmund.

Hannah returned her gaze to her future husband, sensing the vulnerability lurking behind his proud stare.

She yearned to know what had happened to him, what had caused such scarring, and how he had survived it. She knew he had fought in the war, knew he had been injured, but hadn't been aware of the extent of it. No wonder he had hidden himself away far from London.

Despite his lack of greeting and his fierce scowl toward them all, Hannah's instincts told her that she was better off marrying a man like this than Lord Marshville, who would have left her bed for another right after the vows were spoken – never mind the warnings she had been provided at the party. A part of her still longed to wait until she learned the identity of her mysterious stranger from the library, a man she had been unable to push from her mind, but in all likelihood, she would never see him again.

This was her future now, and the best way forward was to begin as optimistically as possible.

"Yes," she finally said, speaking for them all. "Let us begin."

ONE THING EDMUND could say about his new wife was that she was much braver than she looked.

He stole a glance over at the carriage trundling alongside him. For the first part of the journey, she had kept the curtain pulled back, peering out the window as though taking in everything that passed outside. He had hung back then, not wanting to obstruct her view.

He guessed she was likely sleeping now, for there hadn't been any sign of her for some time.

His heart constricted as he thought of her. What would she say if she knew he was the man she had kissed that night, that his scarred face was the one that had brushed up against hers in the dark?

Edmund had seen the shocked expression upon her face when he entered the doorway of his parents' sitting room, had noted her mother's gasp and the denial that was forming on her father's lips. But then Hannah had stepped forward, shoulders up and head held high, bravely declaring that she would go on with the wedding.

He had to admit that part of him was hoping she would cry off.

The other part despaired at any thought of her doing so.

For she stirred something within him that had been lying dormant for a very long time now. He hadn't even known that such desires were possible for him anymore, not since... since the war. How long had it been since he had been with a woman? Over six years now, he mused. He had tried – once. The prostitute had come into the room and taken one look at him before nearly fainting dead away. She had tried to up her rate, but by that point he no longer had any interest in whatever favors she might provide and he had sent her away.

He had never tried again.

Now he had a wife. He took a deep breath. This was the last thing he had expected when he had made the trek to London for his brother's engagement and ensuing marriage. As much as he never wanted this and knew they could never truly be husband and wife, at the very least she was safe from his brother.

But, he thought as they crested one hill and he saw the approaching inn in the distance, was the danger with *him* far worse?

HANNAH HADN'T KNOWN what to expect from her husband. But she hadn't expected this silence.

He hadn't looked at her once through the wedding. When he had repeated the few words required of him, his voice had sent shivers down her spine. There was something terribly familiar about it, and she searched her brain for when she might have met him before.

"Never," he had said tersely when she had asked him, and so she had pushed the thought away, although something about him nagged at her, something she couldn't quite determine. It was quickly overcome, however, by her ire that he had refused to wait for her to prepare for the wedding, but had been determined to have it over with quickly so that he could return to his beloved home. It must be quite something.

She had said a quick, tearful goodbye to her parents, though her sadness had acquired a bitter edge when she saw her father and Lord Heatherstone shake hands as though they had just finished conducting a successful business deal – although to them, she supposed this was exactly what it was.

She and her maid, Molly, had been deposited into the carriage, and before she could ask where her husband was, the door had been shut and she had been sent on her way. Had she not seen him riding beside the window, she would have wondered whether he had even accompanied her.

He rode with his collar lifted high and his hat pulled low, hiding himself from the world. It was interesting. The man who had approached them so proud, so defiant must be in there somewhere, and yet he lived within a fortress he had erected around himself.

He had secured separate rooms for them at the inn, and had arranged for trays to be brought up to them. He hadn't said a word to her, beyond knocking on her door the next morning and calling out the time they were to depart.

Hannah didn't know what to think of it – or what to think of *him*. She was quite aware that he hadn't asked to marry her, and she wondered if he planned to spend the entirety of their marriage like this. Her stomach rolled at the thought.

"What do you suppose Hollingswood to be like, my lady?" her maid asked her during the journey.

"I don't know, Molly," she said, attempting to mask her own anxiety at the thought of it, "but I think we're about to find out."

It seemed as though the horses picked up speed as they neared the manor. Hannah practically fit her body through the window as she stretched out her neck to see what was before them, but in doing so she nearly lost her head.

The vegetation had become quite thick around them, the road narrow and bumpy. It was as though hardly a person ever travelled this road, and despite it being midday, all Hannah could see was darkness within the depths of the trees.

She couldn't see Edmund anymore. He must be either in front of or behind the carriage, and Hannah shivered as she wondered what lurked in the trees. She sat back down, pulling the curtain closed once more.

"It's creepy out there," Molly said, and Hannah didn't answer, not wanting to show any fear, despite the fact she wholeheartedly agreed.

Finally, the carriage began to slow while Hannah's heart picked up speed as she prepared to see her new home for the first time.

She slowly descended the carriage steps, nearly missing

the last one as her attention was focused on the estate before her.

If it could be called an estate. That might be generous. Hannah wasn't entirely sure if this was the actual house, or perhaps the ruins of another that had sat here in the past.

The half-timbered building was shaped extremely irregularly, with three different ranges forming what must be a courtyard within. Stone footings seemed to be present at the bottom of the house, while diagonal oak braces created a strange pattern upon the façade. Three chimneys, surrounded in brick, rose at varying levels, and pointed arches topped the doorways on two of the sides. Moss crept up the walls, as though nature was attempting to take it over once more.

Most shocking of all was the little moat that surrounded it.

"It's..." Hannah was lost for words.

Edmund dismounted and passed by her, not even pausing as he answered, "It's home."

4

He never should have brought her here.

Hell, he never should have married her. But after that, he should have given her his name and allowed her to stay in London, with her family. That, however, would cause such scandal, especially after all that had occurred with his brother. He didn't want to put her through that once more. Best to take her here, hide for a while, and then return her.

Edmund knew he should walk her inside and provide her with a tour of the place. But, he figured, it was best to allow Mrs. Ackerman to do it. He knew his wife would likely feel far more comfortable with his housekeeper than she would with him. He had seen the way she looked at him, with such trepidation on her face. She was likely worried about the anticipated intimacy between them. But she shouldn't be worried. He had no plans to assume his husbandly duties.

"Dinner will be at eight," he called over his shoulder as they entered the hall, before he continued upstairs to his bedchamber to wash himself for dinner.

He was an ass. He knew that.

But better an ass than a fool. He entered his room, the grate dark as his staff wouldn't have known his arrival time, although he had written ahead to advise that he would be appearing much sooner than they would have expected him.

He realized that he had forgotten to write about his wife. Well, Mrs. Ackerman would take care of that. Edmund walked toward the window to look out on the dense wood beyond, but as he did, he caught sight of himself in the mirror – a mirror that he kept only because he had no valet, and at times he had to ensure he was dressed appropriately. Usually, however, he kept the mirror covered in thick black cloth, but somehow it had come askew and was pooled on the floor.

For every time he caught sight of himself, he was horrified anew at just how terrifying he looked – at least from the left. How had Hannah brought herself to stand next to him to be married, when he couldn't even look at himself in the mirror?

He grimaced and sank down at the bed, unable to stomach staring at himself any longer, and yet equally unable to look away.

Finally, he stood up and threw the black cloth over the mirror once more, deciding that he wouldn't be going down for dinner.

He would allow the woman to eat without his terrible visage staring back at her.

It was the least he could do.

HANNAH HAD STOOD in front of the house, unable to move. To enter, they had to cross over the moat upon a small bridge, passing through what she took to be a gatehouse. When her steps had faltered within the courtyard as she stared up at the house, her husband had continued on, leaving her beyond to discover the secrets for herself.

Marrying Edmund Marshville in the drawing room of his family's London home had seemed an easy decision. But suddenly, as she stared at the entrance to the home, it all sank into her, and she began to involuntarily tremble as a chill ran down her spine.

Molly said nothing, but she brought her hand up to rest on Hannah's back, and at that moment, Hannah had no care in the world that the girl was her servant. She turned around and clung to Molly's hand, staring at her beseechingly.

"Thank you for coming with me, Molly," she said, her eyes filling with tears at her gratefulness, and Molly nodded, though her own smile seemed rather forced.

"The house might be an interesting subject to paint?" she said hopefully, and Hannah smiled in thanks at her attempt at levity.

They stepped through a porch and screened passage, although the screens were missing, and the porches were decorated in elaborate carvings.

Her husband now completely disappeared, it seemed that no one was here to greet them but the house itself, which seemed to begrudgingly welcome her into its bowels.

She looked around the great hall in wonder, mesmerized by all it held within. The floor was flagged, embers in the central hearth providing little heat and a slight bit of light, which also entered through the gabled bay window that looked out over the courtyard. A doorway led to another room beyond, and Hannah could see a staircase leading up, though she had no idea whether she was supposed to follow it or not.

Molly was circling the room, trailing her fingers along the wall. She looked across what seemed to be a dining room table at Hannah, her eyes wide.

"This house must be centuries old," she said with wonder, and Hannah nodded in agreement.

They both jumped when there was a crash from the room beyond, and Molly quickly hurried over to join Hannah. They stood there in the middle of the room, nearly squeezed together, as shuffling footsteps sounded beyond the entrance.

"Who is there?" a voice demanded before they saw anyone, and both Hannah and Molly jumped again. Hannah realized she had grasped Molly's hand in hers and was squeezing it hard.

Hannah opened her mouth to announce herself, but then realized she had no idea just how to do so anymore. Finally, a figure appeared in the doorway. The woman's shoulders were somewhat stooped, her hair gray, her glasses low on her nose.

"Who are you?" she said now, pushing her spectacles up as though to better see Hannah.

"L-Lady Hannah," she finally managed. "I am..." she exchanged a look with Molly. "I am Lord Edmund's wife."

The woman stopped, not moving for what seemed to be a full minute.

"Well, I'll be," she murmured, then placed her hands together in front of her chest and looked up, her lips moving in an apparent prayer. "I wish I had known you were coming."

Hannah nodded. She wished she had known as well.

FOR A HOUSE THAT SEEMED SILENT, it certainly held many noises.

Hannah wished she had more chance to explore it, but Mrs. Ackerman had been quite busy preparing a room for her. Hannah also wished she had insisted that Molly remain with her, but Mrs. Ackerman had been adamant that the servant's quarters were below. Hannah had a hunch that the housekeeper had done so with the notion that Hannah would expect time to be with her husband, but the man couldn't even bring himself to have supper with her.

Hannah was more than aware that he hadn't wanted to be married. But this seemed to be quite beyond what she had anticipated.

Her room was cold, despite the fire that was burning in the stone fireplace on the far wall. There was simply no decoration and no life to it beyond the panels on the walls, although they only further reminded her of the many people who had lived and died here over the centuries. She closed her eyes, breathing deeply as she told herself to take this one day at a time. For if she began to remind herself that this was her entire future stretching out in front of her, panic began to build in her chest that she didn't know how to tamp down.

After what seemed like hours, her eyes finally began to drift closed, until a soft keening from down the hall reached her ears, and her eyes snapped open as she burrowed deeper within the blankets.

It must be the wind rustling over the roof of the house, she told herself. Except that she was currently on the first floor, and there was still a story above her. Hannah swallowed hard as the keening turned into a moaning, until an agonized cry rang out.

Chills rushed through her anew, but Hannah told herself that the only explanation was that the sound was coming from a human – although what could be befalling him or her, she had no idea.

But clearly the person was in pain. She wondered if there was anyone here besides Edmund and the servants. She hadn't seen any sign of them, but then, she wouldn't have believed Edmund lived here either had she not seen him enter the house.

She took a breath, steeling all of her nerves to go and see what she could do to help the poor soul.

Finding her wrapper within her as-of-yet unpacked bags, for Molly hadn't had time to put anything away once the room was prepared, Hannah threw it around her shoulders, took up a candlestick, and pushed open the door.

Her bedroom led out to a small balcony which overlooked the great hall. To her left was a staircase; to her right, a closed doorway. She had no idea where it led.

"Hello?" she called out softly, hearing the noises continue from within. She knocked hesitantly on the door, staying back from the railing, the great hall below her a dark abyss.

There was no answer, however, and she placed a hand on the doorknob, unsure of whether she should risk opening it.

But a loud thrashing and shout solved the problem for her, and she threw open the door but stepped back, with thoughts of protecting herself from the unknown entity within.

Her small candle cast just enough light into the room

that she could see a shape underneath the bedcovers, tossing and turning with great agitation.

"Edmund?" she called out, but he still didn't respond. She took hesitant steps toward the bed, finally stopping when she was beside him. His brow was covered in sweat, his hair now unbound, long upon his pillow.

"Edmund?" she repeated, this time reaching out a hand and placing it upon his brow. He stilled at her touch, and she expected him to fling open his eyes and ask her what she was doing there. But he didn't. Instead, it seemed that she had stilled something within him, for his body went slack, and his head lulled to sleep once more. As his features softened and the noises ceased, Hannah became aware of the feeling of his rough skin beneath her fingertips. It intrigued her, and yet she could tell he had no wish to speak of what had happened to him.

She gazed down upon this stranger that was now her husband, wondering at the nightmares that haunted him. She could only imagine the horrors of war he had faced, and wondered if he would ever get over them, or if he would ever share what it was that tortured him so.

Did she even want him to? If she could ease his pain, she decided, then it would be worth it. It would have to be.

He looked so serene in sleep that it seemed a wonder that he was the same man she had encountered before. She wondered anew at just what had actually convinced him to wed her.

Well, she had no desire to have married him either – or his brother. She had been a pawn in a game played by their fathers who were supposed to love and protect their children, but who actually were only looking out for themselves.

She picked up her candle, eager now to return to her

room, for the sympathy that was rising within her was causing her to nearly forgive the way Edmund had treated her earlier. He might not have wished to have married her, she reminded herself, but he should still act the gentleman.

Well, all she could do now was to get some sleep and wait to see what the morrow might bring.

As she returned to her room, she couldn't shake the sense that someone was watching her.

It's just the house, she told herself, attempting to be reasonable.

But that didn't stop her from running as fast as she could through the door, slamming it behind her, and jumping under the covers as though they would save her from all the unknown that threatened.

It wasn't reasonable.

But it was instinct. She had relied upon it when it told her to marry Edmund. She could only hope that she could still trust it. Because right now, it was all that she had.

5

Hannah decided that if no one was going to provide her with a tour of her new home, she would just have to embark on one herself. She began in the great hall, where they had found themselves the previous day. Only now, with exploration in mind, she noticed the dragons carved into the arch-braced trusses above, as well as the service wing that was connected to it.

"The little parlor is through here."

Hannah jumped, bringing her hand to her throat as she turned to find a middle-aged man standing in the doorway across the room. He was rather attractive, his hair a sandy brown just beginning to turn to gray.

"You startled me," she said, as her pulse began to return to its normal beat.

"My apologies," he said, though he didn't seem particularly contrite. "I'm Falton, the butler. Well, butler, groom, footman, gardener – all except housekeeper, cook, and maid, which falls to Mrs. Ackerman."

"Are there no other servants?" Hannah asked wonderingly.

"No," Falton said, shaking his head. "Lord Edmund primarily takes care of himself and does much of the work as well. Doesn't want many about."

"I see," Hannah murmured. "Do you happen to know where my husband is at the moment?"

A ghost of a smile played at Falton's lips. "Not particularly. If it's not too forward, my lady, I must say that your arrival was certainly a surprise to us."

"To me as well," Hannah said, considering that it was Edmund's place to tell his staff the story of their marriage. "I don't suppose you could provide me with a tour?"

"I'd be happy to," Falton said with a nod, holding a hand out toward the room he had named the parlor. "This way."

Hannah followed him into the small room. Painted paneling that looked as though it had been part of the house for all of its centuries covered one wall, and she walked closer toward it in order to get a better look.

"We believe it was painted to look like marble," Falton said. "The drawings are crude, but they tell the story of Susanna and the Elders from the Apocrypha."

"Incredible," she said, and it was. Hannah tried to picture the hand that had painted these so many years ago, wondering what joy they had found out of this painting upon the wall. She followed Falton through the sparsely furnished parlor, passing another staircase to an adjoining room.

"This is the withdrawing room," he said, and Hannah stood in the doorway, shocked to find the room completely stark, but for the carved wooden paneling and the wooden ceiling with molded coffering. "Lord Edmund doesn't see the need for an additional room in use," Falton said, "so this remains empty."

"What is through this door?" she asked, crossing over to it, but Falton hesitated.

"Perhaps, my lady—"

But Hannah had already opened the door, her eyes widening when she glimpsed the room within.

Bookshelves covered the walls, with one side nearly bare but for the sizeable bay window with a rainbow of stained glass that would be beautiful when the sun shone through it. A chimneypiece was decorated with female caryatids and the arms of Elizabeth I; the plaster bore remnants of the original paint and gild. Hannah imagined that at one time it had been quite beautiful – in fact, the same could be said of the entire house.

The furniture in the room was dark, though it looked comfortable. On one wall between two bookshelves hung a painting of a man that bore an uncanny resemblance to Edmund, though Hannah could tell that while he held his likeness, it wasn't her husband depicted on the canvas. He was older than Edmund currently was, and it couldn't have been painted before he had left for the war.

"Who is that?" she asked, walking over to the painting, lifting a hand to touch the canvas.

"My great-uncle."

Hannah whirled around at the low, gravelly voice, finding the silhouette of her husband standing in the doorway.

"Edmund," she greeted him, though she couldn't help the hint of reproach in her tone. Her husband had deposited her here in this house and then left her for nearly an entire day. "Where have you been?"

"Around," he said nonchalantly. "Does it matter?"

"Of course it does!" she exclaimed.

"I don't make the best of company," he said, stepping

into the room, and Hannah was shocked that when he stood looking out the window, with only his right side visible to her, there was not even a hint of his scar. And yet, the air of an injured man hung around him.

"Some company is better than no company," she said, but he snorted as though he did not completely agree on that count. "Would you continue the tour?"

"Me?"

"Well, you seem to have dismissed my tour guide."

"Very well," he said begrudgingly. "If you've seen the ground floor, then we'll continue upstairs."

He led her out a separate door into the courtyard, which, despite Falton's claim to be the gardener, looked like it could use a great deal of care. She was surprised when a small entrance led to an additional stairwell.

"How many staircases are there?" she asked.

"Four in total," he replied, and she held on tightly to the railing as the narrow wooden stairs were not particularly even. Like the other staircases, it curled round until they reached the first floor. "We are on the opposite side of your bedchamber," he said, admitting that he at least was aware of where she slept. She couldn't help but note how tall he was, his frame lean and wiry, far from the usual for a nobleman. He wore no cravat, the top buttons of his shirt open. He reminded her more of a laborer, and she wondered at Falton's words that he enjoyed doing much of the manual work himself.

"The garderobes are through here," he said, pointing. "If you continue on to the far end, you will reach the servants' quarters. These rooms would be for guests... if we were to ever have any."

A pained expression crossed his face, as though he realized it might be a possibility now that Hannah lived here. They crossed through a room he told her was the guests' hall, though all of the furniture was covered in sheets and blankets.

"This is a prayer room," he said, walking into the next chamber, then laughed wryly before continuing on.

"What happened?" she asked softly, stopping in the sparsely furnished room.

He looked back at her over his shoulder, his scars shining in the light of the windows. "Excuse me?"

"I asked what happened?" she repeated, keeping her voice gentle. "What has caused you such pain?"

"I was wondering how long it would take you to ask about my scars," he said, and she shook her head.

"I meant the scars within you, although I am assuming they are related."

He turned from her, not making eye contact anymore.

"I was in the war."

"I know."

"I was shot," he said, his words clipped, as though even saying them aloud brought back the pain. "Twice. I was taken prisoner."

"For how long?" she asked, not wanting to hurt him but sensing that it would be best if he talked about it aloud.

"Just over a year."

"Oh, Edmund," she said, not able to imagine it.

"It's over now," he said, only, she could tell that it wasn't – not for him. She didn't want to think of what horrors he might have sustained, and to be in enemy territory with such an injury... no wonder it looked as it did. It probably hadn't been properly cared for.

"We keep these rooms here open, in case we do ever need them," he said, dismissing the other topic. "There is a small passage that will take you to the other side, where your bedroom is... and mine."

She nodded, wondering if he was pleased that she was so close to him, or if it had been Mrs. Ackerman's doing. He didn't exactly seem thrilled by the prospect.

"And the upper floor?"

He seemed to hesitate, before he finally led her to another staircase.

"Come."

EDMUND HAD TOLD himself to stay away from her.

But when he had seen her standing in the door of the library – the room that was *his* more than any other in this house – he hadn't been able to keep himself away. He was drawn to her, almost as though she was fey with the ethereal quality that radiated around her. She was a bright light in this dark house, and yet somehow... it seemed as though she belonged, like Hollingswood had opened up its arms and accepted her as part of it.

He was waiting for her to insist that he return her to London, that she couldn't stay any longer in this house, or with him, but so far, she simply seemed curious.

Well, at some point that curiosity would subside and she would be ready to return, away from all of this.

"My goodness," she said, taking a breath as they reached the top floor. "What room is this?"

"This is the long gallery," he said. "As you can see, it is not exactly a paragon of architectural prowess."

The floor was warped and wavy, the walls leaning inward and outward at various angles. It was long and crooked, with crossbeams between the arch-braced roof trusses that were likely added at some point in order to keep the structure from coming down around them.

"What is it for?" she asked, walking along the corridor, running her fingers along the windows that lined the room.

"Perhaps a gallery or a games room," he said with a shrug. "It has never contained much furniture. At the end, you will see plaster depictions of destiny and fortune."

She reached the north wall, whispering the words. "The wheel of fortune, whose rule is ignorance," she read off of the inscriptions. "The sphere of destiny, whose rule is knowledge."

She turned to him. "What do you think it means, that someone would believe so strongly in these words to inscribe them on the wall?"

He wasn't sure, but he followed her, standing next to her, reaching his fingertips out to the inscriptions as well. Her hands looked so small, so pale, and he longed to reach out and clasp them in his own. When her fingertips brushed against his as she moved her hand back, a shock from her warmth ran through him and he stepped back abruptly away.

"There's one more room," he said gruffly, the door creaking open when he pushed against it. "This is the upper porch room."

"It's a bedroom," she said, wondering at the fact it was still furnished.

"It has been for some time," he said, as she walked over to inspect the fireplace. Here, the figures of justice and mercy adorned it.

"Does anyone frequent this floor?" she asked. "This may sound silly, but it seems to be occupied. The objects in this room—" she pointed to a quill pen, inkwell, and vellum laid out on a writing desk "—do they belong to someone?"

Edmund hesitated. He wasn't entirely sure how to explain it, and he didn't want to give her another reason to leave. Despite the fact he knew she would go at some point, he wanted to delay her departure as long as he could. Which was ridiculous. He wanted to be alone, had no desire to ever marry. So why did he yearn for her presence?

"They *did* belong to someone," he said slowly. "You saw my great-uncle's portrait downstairs?"

She nodded.

"He was also the second son. This was his home. He loved this room, with its view upon the gardens below. At one point in time, there was a beautiful knot garden just beneath these windows. You can still see traces of it today. Anyway, these are his things. He moved to this room because... well, because he could see out to the guest house beyond, where his brother and his wife would stay when they visited. When he died no one ever had the heart to remove his things. Now they seem to be part of the home." He turned to Hannah. "You see, he loved his brother's wife, his Isabel, and she died here as well."

Hannah's eyes had grown even wider as he had told the story, and she stared at him incredulously. "Do you think her spirit is still here?" she said in a whisper, and Edmund shook his head – not because he didn't want to scare her, but because he believed in what he said.

"No, she isn't here," he said, then regarded her for a moment, wondering if she could handle what he had begun to realize as the truth. "I think that's the problem."

6

"The problem?"

Edmund nodded slowly at her words, and Hannah leaned in closer toward him, needing to know more.

"At times I sense... well, I sense that my great-uncle's spirit *does* remain," he said, before one side of his lips curled up into a self-deprecating smile. "Which is foolish, I know. There are no such things as spirits. And yet, I get the sense that someone remains here, waiting. I think he's waiting for her."

"Why did she marry his brother?" Hannah asked with a frown, and Edmund sighed.

"I don't know if they fell in love before or after. They likely didn't have much choice."

"Oh." A feeling of knowing settled over her. "I see."

"I don't know for certain that they ever acted on their feelings," Edmund said, turning from her, "just family rumors."

Hannah could sense he didn't want to talk about it

anymore, and she opened the top drawer of the desk. "Is there anything else in here?"

Edmund was still staring out the window, his hands in his pockets, when she looked over at him.

"I'm not sure," he said. "I've never looked. I didn't know if it was my place."

He was right. And yet Hannah had the strange idea that it *was* her right, that no one – spirits or otherwise – would mind if she opened this drawer to determine what was within.

She had to give it a hard tug to bring it out, and a musty odor wafted up from within, as well as the stale scent of dried roses.

"A rosary," Hannah said, finding what had slid around when she had opened it. "One of them was Catholic."

There wasn't much else – a handkerchief, a watch fob, and a shaving set. She reached her hand in, her fingertips brushing against a stack of papers in the back. She pulled them out, finding them bound with a long blue ribbon.

"Letters," she said, looking up and catching Edmund's startled gaze. "Did you know they were here?"

"No." He shook his head. "I've never seen them before."

She unbound the ribbon, letting it flutter to the floor.

"Do you think it's our place to read them?" he asked, and she met his eyes, taken off guard by their intensity.

"Whose place would it be?" she asked, and he shrugged.

"I'm not entirely sure."

"At least let's see who wrote them," she said, unbinding the first letter, slipping it out of the envelope, whose seal was already broken.

"*My dearest love,*" she read, adding, "It's in a woman's handwriting, I would think. The writing is soft, the letters slanted and looped."

She walked over to the window for better light, her breath catching at Edmund's nearness. His hands were balled into fists at his side, his forearms strong, muscular, his veins nearly popping out of them.

She cleared her throat, looked down at the paper in her hands, and began.

"It is getting worse. I find myself hiding when he returns home from wherever he goes until the wee hours of the morning. The bruises he leaves on the outside are not nearly as bad as those within. I wish I knew what happened to change him so. His anger is volatile, his temper unreasonable. I am trying to convince him that we should come visit you once more. I do long to see you again, though I fear that he will ascertain the feelings we hold for one another if we are all together. Oh, Andrew, I do not know what to do. Please, tell me? Always your love, Isabel."

Hannah was silent for a moment, the pain of the woman's words slicing through her.

"They were in love," Hannah breathed, looking up at Edmund. "And she was in danger. Do you think they fell in love with one another before she married his brother, or afterward?"

"I don't know," Edmund said. "Perhaps the other letters will reveal it. Are they all from her, or are his replies included?"

Hannah shuffled through them. "They look to be all written by her. I wonder if his letters are here somewhere."

"Perhaps," Edmund said. "This house holds many secrets."

"How did she die?" Hannah asked, needing to know.

"In a fire," Edmund replied, wincing at the words, and she wondered if he was remembering his own pain. "At the guest house where she stayed. She was within when it burned down."

Hannah gasped. "That is awful."

"It is," Edmund said grimly. "The ruins are not far – around the wood in the back. I can show you later if you'd like."

Hannah nodded, though her stomach tightened at the thought. "I should see them," she said bravely, "if this is to be my home."

Edmund's blue-eyed stare turned on her, capturing her for more than a moment, and she wondered if she had said the wrong thing.

"Is it not?"

He nodded slowly. "It is."

Hannah was so shaken that when she began to walk toward the door, her toe caught the corner of the low chair and she began to tumble forward. She threw out her hands in order to catch herself, whether on the stool or the bed she wasn't entirely sure, but then strong arms came around her, catching her before she could pitch forward at all.

"Easy," Edmund said, his hands encircling her waist, and Hannah allowed herself a moment to lean into him. A tingle coursed through her at his touch. She couldn't be sure if it was him, or the fact she had never been so close to a man — besides her library stranger — that caused such sensations, but she had to admit that she was becoming quite fascinated by him. He was her husband, and yet she knew nothing about him.

It seemed he enjoyed their closeness as well, for he allowed his hands to linger. When he finally set her back on her feet and moved away, Hannah noticed crisscrossed scars on both of his hands and averted her gaze before he caught her staring.

"I'm so sorry," she said, warmth rising in her cheeks. "I

don't recall the chair being here before. In fact, I'm fairly certain it was tucked underneath the desk."

She pushed it back where it belonged, the sound of the wood scraping against the floor loud to her ears in the silence that had stretched between them.

"Here," she said, handing him the packet of letters, their fingers brushing against one another as she did so. "You should keep them."

"No," he said, wrapping her fingers around them, his hands cold yet somehow sending shocks through her from where they touched. "They remained lost until you arrived. Perhaps it is your role here to unravel this mystery."

"Perhaps," she said. As they walked out of the room and back down the long gallery, Hannah could have sworn someone was watching them.

"You wily old goat," Edmund muttered as he took a seat in his library, pulling out a fresh sheet of vellum as he dipped his quill pen in the inkwell. He looked up at his ancestor, shaking his head at him. Edmund had long accepted the fact that his great-uncle had not yet departed the estate he had called home many years prior. It seemed the spirit was up to some mischief now.

"We are not a love match," he continued, though knew that if anyone walked in upon him speaking to a portrait, he would be considered mad. "It was all a business transaction. That, and preserving my family's dignity. I'll look after the woman, I promise, but I doubt she will remain here long."

A book fell from one of the shelves and Edmund rubbed his forehead over where the scars began. It was always a bit itchy.

"Yes, we will try to solve your little mystery," he promised with a sigh. "But if you continue to spook her, I'm sure she will be gone from here even faster than we were married."

Edmund did dine with his wife that night, though he said little, despite her repeated attempts at conversation. He noted she didn't eat much. Instead, she simply pushed the food around on her plate as though she had no appetite. He looked down at his own dinner. He supposed Mrs. Ackerman was not exactly the most accomplished cook, but he hadn't overly cared. He ate only to sustain himself, not to engage in any culinary delights.

"Perhaps we will have to see about hiring a cook," he muttered, and Hannah looked up at him hopefully.

"That might be nice," she said with a smile, showing off teeth that were just a bit crooked, though somehow they made her much more endearing. She was such a pretty thing that he despaired of the fact her beauty was wasted upon him and this house, away from London and all who would desire to look upon her. She was one of those women who would likely forever seem much younger than she was in reality.

After dinner he retreated to his library to write once more, and she trailed along after him. He supposed she didn't have much else with which to occupy herself.

She stood in front of his bookshelves as he took a seat behind his desk.

"You have quite a collection," she observed, to which he responded with a grunt. "Are they yours, or were they here when you arrived?"

"Both."

"When did you first begin living here at Hollingswood?"

"After I returned from war," he said, not particularly inclined to share details.

"Who lived here before that?"

"Another relative, but he died years before. It was empty for about fifteen years."

"I see."

She wandered closer toward him, looking up at the portrait above him.

"Your great-uncle looks quite a lot like you," she said, tilting her head to study him.

"So I am told."

"Did he have any children?"

"No," he shook his head. "It is how the house eventually came to my father and then to me."

"Was your grandmother Isabel, the woman from the letters?" she asked, and Edmund sighed, raising his head as he gave up all hope of work.

"No," he answered her, looking up and giving her his full attention. "After she died, my grandfather remarried, and they had children together. There were no offspring from his first wife."

"I suppose that is for the best," she said, to which he agreed.

"How long did your great-uncle live?"

Edmund rose now and walked over to her, coming to stand next to her shoulder.

"Not long," he said. "After the tragedy here, he joined the war effort. He was gravely injured, but returned here to die."

"I wonder if he lost all hope of living anymore, after losing his love," she murmured.

"It's not that simple," he muttered, and she turned her wide-eyed stare upon him.

"What isn't?"

"Choosing whether or not to die. Sometimes it is impossible, as much as you will it to be so."

Her gaze turned sympathetic, and he turned away from her pity.

"Why, Edmund?" she asked softly. "Why would you want to die? You have always had much to live for, have you not?"

"It wasn't worth it," he said, shaking his head. "Not where I was."

"I thought prisoners were treated rather well," she said with question.

"Officers often are," he said. "When I was captured, however, it must have been impossible to determine my insignia. I had lost my jacket and my clothing was in ruins. I ended up on a prison depot that was basically forgotten about. Unlike most, it was rife with disease and death. I would likely have faced my end there had not fellow prisoners looked after me. How I survived, to this day I am not entirely sure. I should have died of infection. When we —" he couldn't say it. It was too much to share, "when I was finally rescued and I saw the sun once more, at first I thought I had died and was seeing heaven – until I realized that the chance of me ending up there was so low that it *had* to be reality."

"Oh, Edmund," she said, looking up at him. "I don't believe it. You are a good man."

"How do you know?"

"I just do," she said, looking up at him with such hope, such trust, that he couldn't turn away, as much as he wanted to.

"I'm sorry, Hannah," he said softly.

"For what?"

"For ruining your life," he said flatly. "You did nothing to deserve this – life with me."

"I believe," she said, stepping closer to him, "that this is a far better life than what I would have had with your brother."

At her upturned face, her ill-placed faith in his goodness, he couldn't help himself. He raised his hand to her soft skin, gently brushing his fingertips across it. It was as smooth as the finest silk gown. And when she stood on the tips of her toes and brushed those lips he remembered so well against his, he was lost.

7

Hannah hadn't meant to kiss him.

Or, maybe, deep within her, there had been a part of her that had wanted to. But she couldn't recall making a conscious choice to press her lips against his.

Edmund was surly. He was gruff. He *chose* to be closed off from her and the rest of the world.

But his vulnerability, however much he attempted to hide it, was obvious. She wanted to know the man who was hidden underneath, the man he surely had been before he had gone off to war and nearly died.

He hadn't seemed inclined to share, but when their lips met, it seemed that all of the emotion he had been hiding deep within came pouring out through where they were connected.

It began as a chaste, quick meeting of the lips.

Then, with some hesitancy, they started to explore one another, their lips moving over each other first in soft, quick kisses, until the pressure increased and they melded into one.

The dance then began as Hannah sensed something change within Edmund, and as one of his hands came behind her head, the other pressed against the small of her back, holding her close as he tasted and touched, until his tongue dove against the seam of her lips and she opened to him.

It was then, as he kissed her in earnest, when she nearly lost all ability to breathe, that she *knew*.

She stood as still as a statue as the realization poured over her, so much so that he released her when she quit responding to his touch.

"What's wrong?" he asked gruffly, and while Hannah knew he was likely assuming the very worst, she couldn't speak for a moment.

He said nothing as he stepped back away from her, walking around her as he made his way to the door.

"Goodnight," he said, his words so low she almost couldn't hear them, but she managed to find her voice before he left the room via the closest staircase in the back corner.

"It was you."

He stopped, pausing in the doorframe.

"What?"

"It was *you*," Hannah repeated, walking toward him now, more astonished than anything else. "The night in the library. The night of your brother's tryst. *You* kissed me. You warned me against him."

She shook her head, feeling the fool. She had known that Edmund had seemed familiar – his voice, his stature – but she had thought that she would quite obviously have remembered his face. It was because she hadn't seen him.

"Why didn't you tell me?" she asked now, more curious than anything.

"I didn't think it mattered," he replied, not meeting her gaze.

"Of course it mattered," she said. "I *felt* something that night. I wanted to find you again, to determine if that connection would stand. When we were married, my only hesitation was because of the stranger in the library. And it was you the whole time."

A smile began to spread on her lips, knowing that the man she had feared she had missed was in fact the one with whom she would spend the rest of her life.

"Edmund," she said on a sigh, stepping toward him with the intention to renew their kiss. "Do you know what this means?"

"It means nothing," he said, his voice harsh, cutting through the wistful hopes that had arisen within her. "Nothing at all."

"But—"

"Do not become fanciful, Hannah," he said. "This changes nothing. That night in the library, I warned you off Byron, and I'm glad I did. But you didn't get much of an exchange, ending up with me, now did you?"

"How can you say that?" she persisted. "If you would allow yourself some enjoyment now and again, then—"

"And why should I?" he cut her off, nearly taking Hannah aback by the anger within his eyes. But she would not be intimidated.

"Isn't the better question, why should you not?" she countered. "I cannot even begin to imagine what it must have been like in the prisoner camp, or how much pain you must have endured. But isn't that more reason to provide yourself with the ability to enjoy the life you were given once you were freed?"

He turned abruptly and walked away from her, crossing

the room to stand before the stained-glass bay window, looking out toward the inky darkness beyond.

"There was a man in the prison who took care of me," he said, and Hannah remained rooted to the spot, sensing that he was telling her something he had not shared with another.

"He sounds kind," she said softly, urging him to continue.

"He was a physician," he said, beginning slowly, "had a wife at home, two children and hopefully one more waiting for him, as his wife was expecting another child when he left. He had no reason to enter the war, except that he felt like he wasn't doing all he could for his country. Ended up at the prison. He took care of me, brought me back to life. We spent countless days and nights upon that floating prison of death. He did all he could for those around us, but without any instruments or medication, there wasn't much he could do. Then one night we heard gunshots from the shore. Shouts, metal clanging, horses neighing. The English had arrived, and there was a battle just beyond us. We sat there, hopeful, and when we heard footsteps above us, the first joy we had felt in months intruded as we thought that they had boarded in order to free us."

He was silent for a moment and Hannah said nothing, sensing that he was no longer in the room, but instead back in that prison, reliving the tale.

"We were wrong. It was the French. Just a few of them, but they had arrived to make sure we would never be freed. Started killing us off, shooting us one by one. The man – the doctor? He was shot and fell right on top of me. They never knew I was there, and when they left, I was the only one still alive."

Hannah swallowed hard, a heavy weight filling her

stomach at the thought of him lying there beneath the body of another, of being surrounded by death and able to do nothing but wait for his own end or discovery.

"The English finally boarded, but it was too late – for everyone but me. I spent another year in an infirmary. Falton was in the bed beside me."

He finally turned around, his face haunted, his one good eye boring into her as despair filled it. The scarred side of his face stood out in the glow of the wall sconce from the right side of the room.

"This explains the nightmares."

"You know about them?"

She nodded, and he looked even more pained.

"Why, Hannah?" he asked, his voice pleading, haunted. "Why was I spared when the rest of them – good men, like the doctor, who had people who loved him waiting for him – were taken?"

Hannah finally moved, crossing the room slowly, carefully, so that she wouldn't scare him, as though he was an injured animal waiting for her.

"I don't know," she said softly when she finally reached him. "I wish I did. I wish I knew why there are such atrocities in the world. But the truth is, Edmund, no one knows. The only thing that is certain is that you must live the life you were given. Live it well, for all of those men who never came home. That physician, he wouldn't want you to spend the rest of your life as though you were as dead as he is, would he?"

Edmund said nothing, though his eyes were tortured as he stared at her.

"I don't know, Hannah," he muttered, "I really don't."

For a moment, she wondered if he was going to come to her, to allow her to comfort him and hold him as she longed to. But instead he took a step back, and then another, until he was nearly at the staircase. He took one long, final look at her.

"Goodnight, Hannah."

≈

EDMUND WOKE the next morning with the feeling that the house was closing in on him. He had to get out, to assume some sort of physical activity, or he thought he would truly go mad.

He didn't see Hannah, didn't tell her where he was going. He knew she wanted a tour of the ruins, but he didn't have it within him to see her again. He had told her far more than he'd meant to last night. He couldn't remember making a conscious decision to share any of it with her, but he needed her to understand just why he could never be the man she wanted him to be.

The nightmare had come again, as it always did when he revisited the hell he had existed in for far longer than one should. He could feel the effects of a short, restless sleep this morning.

Edmund considered saddling his horse for a ride, but decided instead to go round to the back and split wood for the fires. The physicality of it would certainly allow him to expend all of the pent-up frustration within him following his conversation with Hannah last night.

He had just carried over a thick branch, setting it down as he hefted the ax once more, when a scream split the air. The ax swung down, splitting the log, before Edmund tossed it to the side and took off at a run, his heart beating faster than if he had sprinted across a field. The scream must have been from Hannah. What could have happened to her? His mind raced with possibilities, of the moat, of the forest beyond — until he realized that he was headed in the direction of the ruins.

He shouted a curse as he realized that she must have gone to explore them herself. He was a fool, allowing his pride to get in the way of his promise to her. He hadn't thought to warn her of the ruin's crumbling walls and roof, of flooring that was liable to give away at any moment. Hell, he hardly ventured within them himself. A woman as slight as her had no business going in there. If he had been with her, he would have ensured she stayed on the outskirts. Now... but there was no time for additional self-recrimination, he told himself as he rounded the corner of the thick brush of trees and came to a skidding halt.

There was dust in the air, swirling around Hannah as she stood there in the midst of the ruined guesthouse. At first glance, it appeared that she was unharmed, and he breathed a sigh of relief as he slowed to a halt, his hands coming to the tops of his thighs.

"Hannah!" he called, and she whirled around toward him, her unbound golden-brown hair flying around her as she did so. He walked toward her, stopping at the edge of the ruin, not wanting to cause any more damage.

"What are you doing here alone?" he called out, more recrimination in his voice than he had meant – recrimination that should be reserved for himself. Why had he not thought to warn her? He had never imagined she would be curious enough to come here alone.

But she was too good to note his unjust reproach, her wide brown eyes shining as she stared at him.

"Edmund, come here. I must show you something," she said, waving him over, and he gingerly began stepping toward her, hoping that he wouldn't disturb anything further.

"Are you all right?" he asked, his breath still coming faster than usual. He wasn't pleased at the panic that had risen within him at the fear of her in danger. Edmund was happy with the way things were. He didn't want to be worried about someone else all of the time, didn't want to care about what happened. For if he cared, then he could lose again, and he didn't think he had anything left within him to break any further.

"I'm fine," she said, wonder in her voice. "I was exploring the ruins of the guest house, and slightly tripped. I put my hand out upon the wall, and it began to give away. The roof above me fell down. It all happened so quickly, but Edmund... something, or *someone* pushed me out of the way."

"What are you talking about?" he asked, narrowing his eyes at her. "There's no one else around. The village is miles away."

"I know," she said with a nod, "it's ridiculous. I can't explain it. I only know what I felt."

Edmund looked around the ruins, though in search of what, he wasn't entirely sure. He hadn't been here in ages. He hadn't seen any reason to. From time to time he walked by it to survey the land, and he supposed that he should have cleaned it up and been rid of it altogether. But something had always stopped him from doing so.

"What's in here?" Hannah asked, stepping deeper into the recess where the wall had fallen away, and Edmund had to surge toward her as he reached out to take hold of her arm.

"Hannah, be careful," he said, the fear leaping up within his throat once more.

"I am," she answered without looking back. "I won't touch anything again, I promise."

He sighed, accepting that she was going to explore this with or without him, so he might as well be there to help her.

It was a small room that seemed to have been preserved despite the fire. He had no idea what it had been – a garderoom perhaps? But before he could give it added consideration, his attention was captured by Hannah's startled gasp.

"Edmund," she said, her voice just above a whisper. "There's something here. It looks like... a music box, perhaps?"

Edmund followed her into the small space, on alert for potential crumbling plaster or uneven footing. He placed a hand on Hannah's waist in order to help her keep her balance. She didn't seem to notice, so intent was she on what was in front of her.

A vanity table sat before them. It was covered in ash, but seemed to have been preserved, protected here in the midst of the destruction around them. On top of it was the music box Hannah had found. She carefully brushed ash and rock off the top before picking it up, blowing additional dust off of it as she tried the clasp.

To Edmund's surprise, it sprang open.

As one, they leaned forward overtop of it, and then shared a meaningful look at the discovery within.

"It's the letters," Hannah whispered, as though they had uncovered a secret for just the two of them. "The answering letters."

"Are you sure?" he asked, not wanting her to raise her hopes. It was true, there was a packet of papers within, wrapped in a ribbon matching those they had found in the manor, but that they could be the matching correspondences...

"I'll take this back with us," she said, reaching for the box.

Edmund shook his head. "We should leave it." But at his words, a piece of the ruins fell outside of the door, and he reconsidered. "Never mind," he said, a chill running down his spine – and he thought he had become rather accustomed to spirits. "We'll take it all."

She nodded in agreement, lifting the box as he took her arm and led her out of the small room and down to the grass below them.

"What do you think the letters were doing there?" Hannah asked, and Edmund shook his head wordlessly, having no idea.

"I had always assumed..." he trailed off, not wanting to speak ill of the dead.

"What is it?" she implored him and he sighed before continuing.

"I had always assumed by the fact that she died there, that it was where Isabel and my great-uncle would meet one another. Maybe she arrived first one night, or he never came, and she ended up alone. I'm not sure if we shall ever know."

"It's so sad," she said with melancholy, and he looked down at her and the wistfulness in her face as she gazed out toward Hollingswood, which loomed before them. "I just wish..."

"What?"

"I wish there could have been a way for them to be together," she continued. "That there was a happy ending, and it all didn't end so tragically."

"That's life for you," he said dryly, and he could tell from her expression that she wished he didn't think such a way, but this was who he was – and nothing was going to change it.

She turned the letters around between her hands, and he could tell how desperately she wanted to open them.

"Would you like to read them together?" he asked reluctantly. The truth was, he was unsure that he wanted to know the ending of the mystery of his great-uncle. For Hannah was right, it *was* tragic, and he had seen enough unhappiness in his time.

"I would like that very much," she said, and he knew he could never go against her wishes.

He nodded, told her they would read them after dinner, and then disappeared inside and to his own rooms.

8

"Hannah," Edmund said as they sat down to eat, each of them accepting a glass of red wine from Mrs. Ackerman, "there is something we must discuss."

"Very well," she said with some trepidation at the seriousness in his tone. The truth was, she was finding it difficult to build up an appetite, for her stomach was swirling with anticipation over the letters. That, and Edmund himself. After their kisses and her realization about who he was, she wondered if there would now be more between them. Should she expect him to come to her tonight? What would she do if he did?

She would accept his touch with the same vigor she did his kisses, she knew. She had drowned within them as though she was a lead weight sinking into him.

Realizing he was staring at her expectantly, she finally returned his statement.

"Yes?"

"You cannot return to the ruins alone again."

"Why?" she asked, narrowing her gaze at him, not appreciating his commanding tone.

"You could have been killed!" he said, his tone harsh as he stared at her, his eyes gleaming in the candlelight, which flickered against the scars of his face.

"But I wasn't," she argued, though that didn't seem to be a solid enough response for him.

"Promise me," he said, his voice gruff, and she fought the urge to cross her arms over her chest.

"You cannot order me—"

"Promise me," he said, his hand curling around his wine glass, the other gripping his fork so tightly his fingers had turned white.

As Hannah stared at him, she wondered for a moment what was causing him such ire. Was it that he didn't want any harm to come to her while she was in his care in case he might be held responsible? For he couldn't care about what actually happened to her – could he? She had thought he might be pleased to be alone once more, to be rid of her and the marriage he never wanted.

"I promise," she said softly, and he nodded curtly before returning to his food. The rest of the meal passed in near silence, as it seemed she had stirred his anger and she worried about saying the wrong thing once more.

Dinner was somewhat improved, which Hannah knew was a result of Molly's assistance with the preparation this evening. When they finished, Hannah stood and walked down the length of the table until she was closer to him.

"Are we still... reading the letters?" she asked, and he nodded.

"I told you we would, didn't I?"

"You did."

"Very well, then."

Hannah reached deep into her pocket, wrapping her hand around the letters, which she had been carrying since she had found them earlier in the day, afraid to put them anywhere else due to fear that she might misplace them before she had the chance to read them.

She followed Edmund into his library, where they would apparently be settling themselves. Hannah was happy about it, for it was where Edmund seemed to be the most comfortable, and the one room that was actually furnished and had the slightest bit of warmth to it.

Edmund gestured toward the sofa near the window, but chilled, Hannah walked over to the fireplace, standing before it with her hands out in front of her. Suddenly softness curled around her shoulders, and she was shocked when she glanced behind her to find that Edmund had placed a blanket around her, though he was now walking away.

"Thank you," she said, and he didn't respond, though he lifted one shoulder in answer. Hannah smiled ever so slightly at his attempt to pretend that it hadn't mattered – but it did. The man who seemed to want all to believe he cared nothing for anyone had noticed her chill. Now that Hannah thought of their conversation at the dinner table, she realized that his order had likely been due to fear for her, and the thought warmed her more than the fire ever could.

"Are you ready to read the first letter?" she asked, and he took a seat in the chair next to her, his long legs stretching out before him.

"If you are."

She nodded, then sat down on the worn yet soft rug below her and reverently pulled out the bundle, sliding one envelope from the package.

He lifted a hand in silent supplication to take the letter, and she nodded, for it somehow felt right that he was the one to read it. He stood and walked closer to the fire for the light.

"*I fear for you. The last time I saw Alistair he was in terrible spirits, his mind muddled and his actions incomprehensible. I despair of the thought of you there alone with him. Come visit, please? I will ensure that he will never know the love we have for one another, but at least here I can protect you. Always your love, Andrew.*"

She slowly raised her eyes to her husband, finding him looking down upon her, his expression unreadable.

"Edmund," she said, her voice just over a whisper. "That could have been me."

"Yes," he said, returning to her and slowly bending to sit and join her on the rug. "You could have been my brother's bride."

"Do you think—" she stopped, for she had never meant to ask the question. It had come to her unbidden, and she had voiced it before she had given any thought to it.

"What?" he prodded softly.

"Do you think that if I had married your brother, that you and I might have come to feel anything for one another?"

He averted his gaze toward the corner of the room.

"You and I hardly know each other," he practically grunted, and Hannah eyed him.

"And whose fault is that?"

"I suppose my brother's," he said, resting his chin on top of his steepled fingers.

"That's not what I meant," she said, playfully slapping his arm in a manner that seemed to surprise him. She wondered when was the last time he had allowed himself to have fun, to not take himself so seriously. "I meant that you continue to avoid my presence as much as you are able to."

"I do not—"

"You do," she said, though the truth was, she couldn't blame him. He hadn't asked for a bride, nor any company at this place where he hid himself away.

"I am sorry, Edmund, for the fact you had to marry me," she said earnestly, in the hopes that he understood her contrition to be true. "I hated being that woman, being paraded about at ball after ball in the hopes that some gentleman might be taken enough with my dowry to wed me, despite what he knew of my family."

"Because of your sister who ran away with the footman."

"Yes."

"Well, I say good for her," Edmund said, surprising Hannah. "And to all the men who overlooked you because of what she did—well, it's their own loss."

Surprise raced through Hannah at his words. "But you didn't want to wed me either."

"That's different."

"How?"

"I didn't want to wed anyone."

"Right," Hannah said, and then they were both silent for a moment, staring at the flickering flames, whose crackling provided the only sound to fill the room for a moment. "Why *did* you agree to marry me?" she finally asked.

She knew she shouldn't have. But the question had been weighing on her mind. For the answer meant more than Edmund could ever know, for it would change everything that was to come between them.

"My father threatened to take away Hollingswood if I didn't."

It seemed like Hannah's heart crumbled into pieces,

with any hopes she had that he had actually felt something – *anything* – for her slipping away.

"Did you—did you know it was me in the library?"

"Of course I did."

"I see," she said, turning away so that he wouldn't see how hurt she was by his words. A part of her had hoped that, perhaps, despite his misgivings toward marriage, there had been something about her that had drawn him into it and convinced him that it might not be so bad.

Apparently, it had only been wishful thinking.

EDMUND KNEW he had said the wrong thing.

But what was he supposed to tell her? He could hardly admit to how much he had desired her, how the thought of marriage to her had not been as objectionable as marriage to any other. For that would be opening himself up to her, leaving him exposed to the rejection that was sure to follow.

"Why..." he didn't want to ask, and yet he needed to know, "why did *you* marry *me*?"

She laughed humorlessly as she stood, wrapping her arms around herself as though she was still chilled, the blanket that he had given her lying discarded on the floor.

"I've always done what I was supposed to," she said, looking down, her voice bitter. "Hannah, the good one. Hannah, who always did what was right. My sister, Justine, she was the rebellious one. It was not a surprise when she ran off with the footman. It was only the latest and greatest scandal. My parents were embarrassed, of course, and despaired for my own marriage. I was never consulted on what I would like. It didn't matter. Then my father worked out an arrangement with yours, and it was apparently all taken care of, until your brother's indiscretion."

She appeared wistful, as she looked up at his bookshelves, at his great-uncle's portrait, out the window – everywhere but at him.

"I wish I could be more like her – my sister. She was rebellious, yes, but she was always so *happy*. She did what she wanted and didn't care about the consequences. Whereas I... I was always so worried about doing the right thing, about being the good girl, about not being contrary. It was almost as though I lived to make up for my sister."

She sighed and looked up at the timbers above her, as though imploring the heavens for an answer.

But unfortunately, the only one here to speak to her was him.

"And now you're here. With me."

"I am," she said, turning to him now, tilting her head as her voice turned contemplative.

"Do you ever wonder... if this is how it is meant to be? If everything happens for a reason?"

"Absolutely not," he said. "That cannot be the case. Not after what I've seen."

She nodded slowly.

"Why do you hide yourself here from the world?" she asked.

"Is it not obvious?" he asked dryly, wondering why she would even need to question it.

"I don't believe it is because of your scars," she said and he stiffened at her analysis of him. "At least, not those on your face. What are you scared of?"

"I am scared of nothing."

"Of rejection?" she continued, as though he hadn't said

anything. "Why do the opinions of those you do not even know matter so much?"

"It is not those that I do not know," he said gruffly, "but those that I do. When I returned from war... do you know how many of my former acquaintances, people I called friends, no longer wanted to have anything to do with me? Who scorned me and were continually busy when it came time to visit? The people who had been my *true* friends – who cared for me, despite what I looked like, what I had suffered, how awful I was to them – were those men who were killed in that prison. The only one who didn't seem to care was in the infirmary bed beside me."

"Falton," she said.

"Yes," he confirmed. "I finally convinced him to come work for me as I learned I could trust him. Plus, he tolerates me. So I have no desire to go out into the world and attempt to create artificial friendships."

She walked over to him, her gaze searching as she looked up into his eyes.

"Don't hide yourself from the world, Edmund," she whispered. Tentatively, she raised one hand up to his face. "And like it or not, I am here now. I have no plans to go anywhere."

Her fingers curled over both sides of his face – the good and the scarred – until they met behind his neck. She interlocked her fingers and then tugged his head down to her.

Why, oh *why* wouldn't she just leave him alone? For the truth was, he was powerless to resist her. He wanted her more than he had ever wanted another – even from long ago, before he had lost all desire.

Or so he had thought.

9

Edmund hadn't known it was possible for a woman's lips to be so plush and soft yet so passionate at the same time. Hannah kissed him with purpose, with intent, as though she was trying to emphasize with her kiss what hadn't gotten through to him with her words.

Edmund wrapped his arms around her waist, tugging her in closer to him. Her soft, lithe body pressed against him, and for a moment, he despaired. It wasn't fair to her, to be left with a man like him, who was broken, scarred, and not even good enough for the prostitute who had scorned him.

But she didn't seem to care. For whatever reason, she was accepting that he was her husband and taking what he had to offer, as dismal as it was.

Edmund caressed her lips with his, grateful that his mouth had been left intact, for he was still able to taste her, to love her with his lips and his tongue, to pour into her all of the emotions that he would never be able to otherwise share with her.

She was so small, yet sturdy, strong, able to carry more of a burden then he would ever want to place upon her.

For he knew that life with him would never be easy. Yet, somehow, she seemed willing to share it, and for more reasons than the simple fact that her parents had decreed it.

"Hannah," he murmured her name as he planted soft kisses upon her lips and her cheeks before tangling his hands in her hair which cascaded down her back. He loved that she wore it down and loose for him, that she didn't keep it knotted on her head all the time. She left him for a moment, running her fingertips down his arms to take his hands in hers as she led him over to the fireplace. She bent and picked up the blanket that lay upon the floor, flattening and smoothing there.

She looked up at him with all of the trust in the world before settling herself on the floor, carefully moving the unread letters to the side in a pile. The firelight flickered off the planes of her face as she looked up at him in supplication.

He knew he could never deny her. She was more than he could ever ask for. More than he deserved.

And everything he thought he would never have in his life.

"We shouldn't," he managed in a husky whisper.

And she answered by widening her eyes and asking, "Why not?"

"Because..." But the truth was, he didn't have much of a reason not to.

"We are married," she said earnestly. "You seem to have some attraction to me."

To that he could only nod, for he didn't think the words for what he thought of her could do her justice.

Suddenly a horrified look came over her face.

"You're not... that is, you weren't injured..." she looked up at him imploringly, as though to ask that he not make her finish the sentence.

He let out a hoarse laugh.

"It all works fine," he said, but then cringed. "At least, as far as I am aware. I haven't, ah... tried it out since returning."

"I see," she said, her innocence showing as her cheeks turned a bright crimson. A log fell over so heavily in the fireplace that they both jumped, and Edmund suddenly realized that by resisting her, all he was doing was causing her to feel unsure about herself, which was so far from his intention.

For the truth was, ever since she had stirred his long-dormant desire in the library of his parents' London town home, he could think of nothing but being with her in every sense of the word.

So finally, for the first time in as long as he could remember, he threw aside the barriers he had erected around himself, and he let go.

He let go of his inhibitions, of his concern over what she might think of him – of his face, of his surliness, of his determination to keep the world at bay.

For right now, all that mattered was the two of them here in this room. She wanted him – he had no idea why – but she did, and all he could do was be as gentle and as loving as he could, to make up for the beast of a man she had married.

He had warring thoughts regarding the light thrown by the fireplace. For while it allowed him to fully see her beautiful, innocent face, he also knew that his own had likely taken on a more shadowy and sinister appearance. The dark would have been preferable, but she needed the warmth in this chilly old house.

Edmund took her lips again as he eased her down onto the blanket before them, his fingers running up and down her arms in a caress. He could sense what might be relief, or possibly even enthusiasm as she softened in his arms, her own hands coming up to pull him close to her.

"Hannah," he said, breaking away from her lips for a moment to look down upon her face, "do you trust me?"

"Yes," she said, her voice just above a whisper, her lips lifting slightly at their corners. "Of course I do."

Protectiveness surged through Edmund at her words. He thought them misplaced – how and why she would put them into a man like him, he didn't know, but he would accept her surrender to him and do all he could to keep her safe and to keep her happy. For that mattered more than anything else ever could.

Hannah began to unbutton his shirt, for he preferred not to wear a cravat at home. Instead, he settled for a shirt and waistcoat or jacket above his trousers. She was hesitant, unsure, but he allowed her to continue, hoping that she would become more confident as she went, though he braced himself for what she would find underneath.

He heard her intake of breath when she had bared his skin to the light, and he looked down to find her eyes filled with sympathy as she shared his pain with him.

"Oh, Edmund," she said, running her fingers over the scars along his chest. "How this must have pained you."

"That it did," he said, taking her fingers so she would leave them be, "but it is over now. They are healed – as haphazardly and disastrously as they may be. Let us focus on the present."

How ironic his words were, for *he* could barely do such a thing, but she nodded, kissing him once more as she pushed the sleeves of his shirt off of his arms. When she lifted it over his head and he was rid of it, he finally began his own exploration. She wore a simple muslin gown, one which she could likely dress herself in, despite the fact that she had a maid.

With his quick tug, the fastenings came loose and the dress began to slip down her slender shoulders. He helped it the rest of the way, before palming one of her breasts in his hand.

She pushed her chest up, clearly enjoying the sensation, which he responded to by leaning down and suckling one nipple through the fabric of her chemise. She breathed in swiftly, holding her breath before releasing it as she kneaded her fingers into his bare shoulders.

Edmund toyed with one of her ankles, beginning to slide his fingers up her leg, but he became so tangled in her skirts that he finally backed away in frustration. She looked up in surprise at his growl, and he tugged off her dress with more ferocity than he had intended. Worried for a moment at what she might think of him, when he looked up at her expression, he found that the corners of her mouth were curled into a smile, as though she had enjoyed the exhibition of his hunger for her.

"I'm sorry," he said, but she shook her head.

"You have no need to be," she responded, looking so small and delicate lying there in just her chemise. "I'm glad to know that you want me."

"Want you?" he said with disbelief. "Goodness, Hannah, that is an understatement if I have ever heard one. Now, come here."

He knelt down by her ankles, slowly crawling up toward her head as he skimmed his fingers over her legs, exploring every inch of her. If he was going to do this, he was going to do it right. She shivered as he knelt, his lips following his hands. He moved over her knee, her thigh, up her hip to her belly, pushing up her chemise as he went. He kissed his way around her navel, up higher and higher until he found her breast once more as he lifted her chemise over her head. Keeping her distracted so as not to scare her, he finally found her center, stroking her, first softly and then with more pressure.

He needn't have worried. As much as Hannah was quite obviously innocent, she more than made up for it with her enthusiasm. She was arching up toward him with eagerness, and suddenly it was as though all that he had been holding within him for six years came rushing forward in anticipation. All of those carnal urges appeared in full force at the demand of Hannah's body.

Edmund wasn't sure how much longer he could wait. But Hannah made the decision for him as she leaned up and unfastened the fall of his trousers. He pushed them off himself, and saw her eyes widen further than he had ever seen them as she took him in.

She said nothing, however, as she seemed to accept that all would be fine. When she reached out and stroked him, he nearly came undone right there, and he closed his eyes tightly and willed himself to wait for her.

"What's wrong?" she asked at what was surely his agonized expression, but he could only shake his head, not trusting himself to say anything. Ensuring she was ready for him, Edmund knelt between her legs, running his hands over her hair to frame her face.

"Are you ready?" he asked, and at her nod, he positioned himself at her entrance and began to slowly ease into her, his own arousal slightly ebbing as he concentrated on her face, ensuring that he was not hurting her beyond what he had to.

She encouraged him to continue with her nod, and he could tell when he broken through her barrier, for she winced. He stilled for a moment and she began to relax around him.

"I'm fine," she said when he didn't look away from her, "truly I am."

He nodded before beginning to slowly retreat and then thrust forward again, and she closed her eyes, tilting her head up as the smile remained on her face. Edmund needed her to finish, for he had no idea how much longer he could wait, and yet he was determined that she enjoy every minute of this. For this was about *her*. Everything was now, he realized. Was this the reason he had lived? So that he could be the man for her, the one who would protect her and take care of her, to show her what it meant to make love, to make her feel as though she was the most important woman in the world?

As he rocked in and out, he teased her nipples, and that was what must have finally sent her over the edge. While her motions stilled, she began shaking around him, squeezing him in such a way that he couldn't help but come himself, pouring into her all of the emotions that he just couldn't say to her aloud.

She looked up at him in wonder, to which he could only offer a breathless grin. Never, in any sort of imagining, would he have guessed that his marriage to this woman would result in a coupling like this, in the possibility of a future of, at the very least, some sort of amiability between them.

Edmund rolled off of her onto his side, turning her so that she didn't have to look at his face and scooping her toward him, his arm coming possessively around her.

As he held her in his embrace, closing his eyes while

nuzzling his nose into her hair, all he could think about was how his life had so drastically changed since his marriage to Hannah.

He had thought he would bring her here, show her what his life was like, and soon enough she would be running back to London, away from him, Hollingswood, and his great-uncle Andrew.

But instead – he swallowed hard as she wiggled against him while making herself more comfortable – he was losing his heart, something he didn't think was whole enough to ever give away.

And the next morning when he woke up in Hannah's bed without any sign of having a nightmare – no twisted sheets, no sweat on his brow, no acknowledgement from Hannah that she had witnessed anything? He knew he was well and truly sunk.

10

annah smiled as she looked around the withdrawing room, which had previously been void of any life or furniture besides the reminders of those who had lived here years prior. Over the past few weeks, with Edmund's permission, she and Molly had converted it into a room of her own. She still spent much time in Edmund's library, but that room would always be his, as much as he was willing to share with her.

Hannah and Edmund had certainly become closer, that much was certain. He was as gruff as ever, but he was slowly showing her the side of him that had previously been surrounded by walls and buried underneath layers.

Hannah looked forward to each evening, when the two of them would sit together and read the letters which had been exchanged between Andrew and Isabel fifty years ago. It was a sad story, that much was for certain.

The south-facing bay window allowed light to flood the room. Edmund had told her that he didn't like her staring at the tragic story crudely painted on the wall, nor the paintings of marble and inlay. He said she deserved a room of marble itself, but in its stead, he had paneled the wall with wood. Having been freshly cut, it beautifully scented the air, and Hannah took a grateful sniff as she turned around the room. It wasn't finished, she knew, though she couldn't quite determine what was lacking.

"My lady?"

Hannah looked up to find Molly in the doorframe. She had been awaiting her to finish with Mrs. Ackerman, and then the two of them were going to go search within the guest rooms to find additional furniture or decoration for the room.

"I'm ready, Molly, if you are," she said.

Her maid nodded in agreement. "I am, my lady."

"How are you finding Hollingswood?" Hannah asked as the two of them began climbing the staircase.

"It's quiet, that is for certain," Molly said, to which Hannah nodded in agreement. "Mrs. Ackerman and Falton are kind, and have been welcoming to me. The house could use a gardener, perhaps, or a footman, particularly if company ever comes."

"I'm not sure that is anything we should be particularly concerned about," Hannah said with some regret.

She enjoyed the solitude and life here away from the city, but that didn't mean she wouldn't enjoy a new face now and again.

Molly nodded, apparently having learned much about her new employer. "I understand that my lord does not enjoy visitors," she said. "I have enjoyed my time in the nearby village when I have my day to myself."

"I must make more effort to get there," Hannah murmured as they rounded the top of the staircase, emerging near the guest quarters on the second floor.

"The villagers would be most interested if you did,"

Molly said. "Lord Edmund is quite the mystery there, and they were all *very* intrigued to learn that he returned home with a bride." She stopped for a moment, intent upon Hannah. "Though I made certain not to share with them anything about you."

"I appreciate your loyalty, Molly," Hannah said with a smile, "and thank you for coming here with me."

Molly nodded as they entered the first chamber. She lifted a blanket off of the furniture, waving a hand in front of her face as dust filled the air. "I *must* speak with Mrs. Ackerman about cleaning out some of these rooms," she said. "I'm sure your parents or your sister will want to come see you at some point, and they must have acceptable living quarters."

Hannah felt slightly uneasy about the thought of Edmund welcoming her family as guests, but she said nothing.

Molly wrinkled her nose in an expression of dismay as she found what was underneath.

"Have a look, my lady, but this is quite dismal," she said, moving from one piece to another. "I think it's best left here."

"There is another room," Hannah said, remembering the upstairs chamber, which Andrew had made his. "It has some beautiful paintings, if I recall. There's also a lamp that could be something we might use, if it is as I remember."

"I've never been up there," Molly said, and she bit her lip worriedly as she lowered her voice as though someone could hear. "I've heard noises, though, coming from above my room at night."

Hannah met her eyes, attempting bravery. She had heard the odd noise herself, but had told herself that it was likely one of the servants. It was also much easier to push aside her worry when she had Edmund's arms around her.

Ever since the night they had first been together, he had come to her for the beginning of the night, though he always left her bed by morning. She had waited for him to have a nightmare such as the one she had discovered him in the throes of during her first night here, but so far, he hadn't woken her. She slept deeply and had no idea how long he stayed with her, but she kept waiting for the day when he would still be snug against her upon the sun's rising.

As of yet, she had been disappointed.

"It's an old house," Hannah said, attempting to reassure herself as much as she did Molly of the strange noises. "I'm sure it's just shifting, or creaking in the wind."

Molly nodded, but Hannah could tell that she didn't quite believe her.

They were silent as they climbed the stairs to the second floor. Hannah led Molly through the long gallery before they stepped through the door into the end bedroom.

"It looks lived in," Molly exclaimed, to which Hannah nodded.

"That's what I said as well," she said. "It hasn't been touched since..." It seemed wrong to share Andrew and Isabel's secret, somehow, even with Molly, "since one of Edmund's relatives lived here."

Molly nodded again before setting herself to the task at hand.

"These draperies are pretty," she said, running her hand over them. "You could use them downstairs. Or perhaps this painting on the wall. It's a beautiful landscape – in fact, it looks like something that could be found near here, although I'm not sure from what vantage." She looked out the window beyond, and Hannah saw she was right.

Far below them, they could see the ruins of the guest house – the reason why Andrew had chosen this room.

"Perhaps the view is *from* the guest house," she murmured. "I shall have to look sometime."

Molly began walking over to take the painting down from the wall, but as she did it fell off on its own, landing at her feet. Molly gasped as she looked up and met Hannah's eyes.

"I... I think we were meant to take it," Molly said, her eyes wide. She bent and picked it up, passing it to Hannah.

Hannah took it in her hands, words on the back catching her eye as she did.

She turned over the painting, reading it aloud.

"*Always my love, Isabel.* She painted it for him."

Molly cast her an inquisitive gaze. "Who?"

"Who... whoever this was," she said, looking forward to sharing her discovery with Edmund. So Isabel was a painter as well. It sent eerie chills down Hannah's spine when she thought of the similarities between the two of them.

She clasped it to her as Molly looked around the room. "Anything else?"

"Perhaps the lamp," Hannah said. "It is nice. And that chair in the corner could work in the withdrawing room, but I'll have Falton or Edmund bring it down."

"Very good," Molly said, seemingly relieved that Hannah was ready to leave the room.

Hannah took a look back, sensing a presence – though somehow, she wasn't frightened. It was as though it was smiling on her, telling her that all would be fine.

EDMUND PAUSED IN THE DOORWAY, looking down on his wife before she knew he was there. She was curled on the settee, reading one of the books she had found in his library. He hadn't told her, but he had always had a feeling it was written by his great-uncle. Edmund had been the one to read Andrew's letters aloud, and he recognized the script. It was eerie, how many similarities he shared with the man. If he hadn't known better, he would have thought Andrew was his director ancestor, as opposed to his own grandfather.

He wished he didn't have to enter and break her solace. But he had news, and it was better she know sooner rather than later.

"Hannah," he said softly, trying not to scare her, but his wife was not one who was startled easily. She looked up at him with a smile, and he wondered whether she knew he was there the entire time and had been allowing him to announce himself at his own leisure.

"Edmund," she said, her voice as comforting and soothing as ever. "What do you think?" She waved her hand around the room, and he was startled to find the painting from upstairs on the wall, in addition to a lamp and a chair that he could only hope Falton had carried down.

"It suits the room," he said in amazement, "as though it was meant to be."

She nodded.

"Look on the back of the painting," she said, and he did as she bid. "It seems that Isabel was a painter too."

"As you are," he said, shock filling him as he looked up at her in wonder.

"Yes," she said, setting her book aside as she stared at him intently. "I know you said that you don't think things are meant to be, but does it not seem like too much of a coincidence, Isabel and Andrew, and you and I—"

"No," he said, shaking his head adamantly. "It cannot be. They ended in tragedy."

"So they did," she said, "but perhaps we are meant to make things right."

"How so?"

"I don't know," she said with a soft laugh. "We are nearly done with the letters."

"We are."

"It's so sad," she said now, quite wistfully. "They loved each other so much. Most of their writings to one another are simply descriptions of what they felt, and a longing to be together. That she had to marry his brother... well, it wasn't fair."

"No, it wasn't."

"And that his brother was so horrible to her... it must have been devasting for him to have to watch it."

"I think that's why he had them stay with him as much as possible. To be close to her, yes, but it must also have been torturous to see her married to another." He could hardly imagine if he had to see Hannah with his brother. "But if she was near, perhaps he was able to protect her as much as he could."

"That's what he says," she agreed with a sigh. "The part about their code, to meet in the guest house when Alastair was in the village..." she didn't mention the part they had assumed, that he was there to find pleasure with the local women, "the light flickering off the mirror as a sign Alastair had gone – it is quite romantic."

"Except for the fact that we know the ending."

That Alastair had learned of the affair and burned the house down, with Isabel still inside.

"Yes," she said, her voice just above a whisper.

"Speaking of brothers..." he said slowly, "my own is coming for a visit soon."

"Here?"

"Yes. Apparently, he wishes to visit before his nuptials."

"But why?"

Edmund didn't like the worry apparent upon her face, and he crossed the room and sat next to her, wrapping an arm around her shoulders.

"Not to worry," he said, "I'll be here with you the entire time he is here. Hopefully, I can quickly ascertain what he wants and then he'll be gone."

"Very well," she said, managing a smile for him, and he tugged his arm tighter around her, his heart reaching out to her when she snuggled in close next to him.

It was on the tip of his tongue to tell her that he loved her, but he couldn't – not yet. For while he thought he did, his emotions had been dormant for so long that he wasn't even sure if he properly understood what the words meant. And so, he stayed silent, content to sit with her and watch the sun set out the window in this room she had turned into one of the most beautiful in the entire house.

That's what she does, he mused, *brings light and life into everything she touches.*

Could she do so for even his dark soul?

11

Hannah sat outside in the back gardens of Hollingswood, painting the landscape beyond – much like Isabel had done so many years ago.

Falton had crafted an easel of sorts for her, and she had taken a stool from upstairs – the very one she had tripped over, causing her to fall into Edmund's arms – and set up her watercolors. She had been remiss from her craft for some time now, so busy she had been adjusting to her new life and preoccupied with the house itself and the letters it held within.

"I'd like to paint the ruins next," she said aloud, and Molly looked at her with some horror.

"Why?"

"Because of all of the secrets they hold," Hannah said. "I'd like to see if I can somehow capture the very essence of them, and not just the eyesore some may see."

Molly shivered. "It's not for me."

"You don't have to come," Hannah said with a smile, which increased when over Molly's shoulder she saw her husband walk out of the back doors toward them.

"Edmund," she greeted him, as Molly nodded at the two of them and then took her leave. "What brings you out here?"

He held up a sheaf of papers, and she looked at him expectantly.

"We haven't read the last letter, and my brother is due to arrive this evening," he said. "I thought perhaps we might finish this first?"

He raised his one eyebrow at her, and she nodded, surprised when he took a seat beside her. She wasn't sure the ground could accurately be called grass, for it had been grown over long ago, but it was certainly an array of vegetation that might be somewhat comfortable.

Edmund opened the letter with his long fingers and began to read. Hannah sat back and simply watched him. It was interesting – she hardly even noticed the scars on half of his face anymore. They were simply part of him, as much as was the burden of guilt he carried around with him over the deaths of all of the men who were with him in that prison.

"Are you listening?" he asked, breaking through her thoughts and bringing her back to the moment.

"Yes, I'm sorry," she said, "can you please continue?"

He nodded.

"*My darling Isabel. It seems strange to write to you when I can look out the window of my bedroom and know that you are but a short walk away. It tears my soul apart knowing that you are there with him, when you will always own my heart. I fear that Alastair has some suspicion of the two of us, and therefore I will stay away. Please, my love, be careful. Give him no reason to doubt you, and if you must, leave and come to me. I will protect you. Always my love, Andrew*"

Edmund looked up at her. "That's the last of it. He was

obviously right. Alastair did discover the truth, and Isabel was taken from him soon after."

He looked out in the distance toward the ruins.

"What are you thinking?" Hannah asked softly.

"Only that I do not know what I would do if something ever happened to you," he said, his voice nearly gutted, so much so that she rose from the stool and stepped closer to him.

"You must not worry. Our situation is much different," she said, standing behind him and wrapping her arms around his neck, "for I know you will always be there for me. The wife you didn't want," she added, teasing him, but he was not in a jovial mood. When he gripped her hands tightly in his, she could sense the desperation within him, though why, she didn't know.

"You feel his pain, don't you?" she asked, and he nodded.

"It is ridiculous, I know, but I feel he is with me... with us," Edmund said. "And yet, I have never been frightened of him."

"No," she said, shaking her head. "It is somewhat... creepy I suppose you could say, that feeling of being watched, but I have no fear."

"He misses her," Edmund said, to which Hannah responded by nuzzling her chin into his shoulder.

"What do you think he is waiting for?" he pondered.

"To be reunited with her, don't you think?" she asked. "It's what I would want. I only wish we knew how to help them."

"Perhaps in time we will," he mused. "I had hoped that by learning their story we might know what to do, but I feel we are no further ahead than we ever were."

"We'll get there," Hannah said, hoping that she could reassure him, "together." She moved to sit on his lap so she could better see his face. "You haven't had any nightmares lately."

"No," he said, a faint smile turning up his lips. "Not since I've been with you."

Suddenly Hannah sensed a presence behind her, and when she turned, this time it was an actual person in the flesh standing within the garden.

"My apologies," Falton said, obviously meaning it, "but Lord Marshville is here."

"Can you tell him we are not home?" Edmund said dryly, and Hannah had to press her lips tightly together to keep from laughing, an action she sensed Falton was mimicking as well.

"He has shown himself into the parlor," Falton said, and Edmund sighed.

"Well, we best go get this over with," he said. "I will speak with him alone after dinner, and then, hopefully, he will be gone."

"Hopefully," Hannah repeated, but a feeling of dread filled her stomach, one that wouldn't go away, no matter how hard she tried.

HANNAH SQUIRMED UNCOMFORTABLY in her seat throughout the meal. Lord Marshville was as she had remembered him – loud, boorish, and quite honestly, rather drunk. Hannah could hardly eat a bite of her dinner, for all she could think about was the fact that she had nearly married the man. How horrible life would have been, she thought, taking a small sip of wine to fortify herself.

She could sense Edmund smoldering from the seat next to her. Instead of sitting across the table from one another,

Hannah had taken to sitting at his right elbow so they could converse through dinner. Unfortunately, tonight Byron sat across from her, and he wouldn't stop staring at her. It disconcerted Hannah, and apparently Edmund was none too pleased as well.

Hannah reached over to him under the table and squeezed his knee.

Byron now looked from Hannah to Edmund and back again.

"So," he said, sitting back and crossing his arms over his chest, "what has kept you two occupied here at Hollingswood?"

Edmund managed a tight smile. "Life, I suppose."

"I don't know how you do it," Byron said, shaking his head. "How dreary it would be, out here in the middle of nowhere. It's a shame to waste such beauty here."

Hannah swallowed hard, looking over to Edmund, for his brother had clearly insinuated just what – or rather who – he was referring to.

"It's interesting, isn't it, that the two of us could have been married?" he said to Hannah with a chuckle. "And now here you are, married to my brother."

"Everything has a way of working itself out," she said, placing her glass down firmly on the table, determined to put this man in his place. She hoped there wouldn't be too many more dinners such as these.

"So it does," he said, smiling sickly at her before he took another sip of his own drink, his gaze not leaving her face.

"I think that's enough for tonight," Edmund said, pushing his chair back and standing abruptly. The fire cracked loudly in the grate through the silence in the room as he stood and stared at his brother.

"We've only just begun," Byron protested, but Edmund shook his head.

"You and I will go to the library to continue this conversation," he said. "Hannah doesn't need to hear it."

"My apologies, *Hannah*, if I have not been a gracious guest," Byron said, slightly wobbly on his feet as he finally stood and began to wander out of the room. "Say, which bedchamber is yours?"

"*Out!*" Edmund commanded, and Hannah didn't think she had ever been so grateful for her husband before.

WHAT EDMUND most wanted to do at the moment was sink his fist into his brother's face and show him just exactly what he thought of his little show back in the dining room.

But if he wanted Byron gone, then he would have to play his little game. He led him into the library, and the door seemed to slam behind them of its own accord. Edmund couldn't help but smile when Byron jumped.

"Sit," Edmund said, but Byron crossed his arms and narrowed his eyes at him.

"I thought I was the older brother here," he said, and Edmund shrugged carelessly.

"That may be true, but you are in my home now," he said. "If there is anything I can actually claim as mine, it is Hollingswood."

"And your wife, apparently," Byron said, finally taking a seat across from Edmund and steepling his fingers together.

"And my wife," Edmund acquiesced, though the truth was he was actually in total agreement regarding Hannah. He didn't, however, wish to talk about her any longer with his brother. "What are you doing here, Byron?"

Byron snorted. "That is quite the welcome."

Edmund leaned forward in his seat. "You have only been through the doors of Hollingswood once before. Why now? Clearly you are after something."

"Well, since I'm here, I did have a favor to ask," Byron said, and Edmund looked up to the ceiling in supplication, though whether he was hoping God or his great-uncle could help, he had no idea.

"Which is..." he asked warily.

"Well, I know your pretty little bride came with a lovely dowry. I know because it was supposed to be mine," Byron said, looking cross. "Since you stole my bride, I believe the least you could do is to provide me with a bit of a... gift, we shall call it, hmm?"

The ire began simmering deep within Edmund's belly, before growing through his chest and then spreading out to his limbs. He set his jaw as he stared at his brother.

"Let me get this right," he said, pointing a finger toward him. "You were betrothed to Hannah, but then you were caught with your pants around your ankles with another woman. When you were forced to marry and give up Hannah, I did what you couldn't. Now you want to take advantage of the money that accompanied her into this marriage?"

Byron cocked his head, and smiled what Edmund was sure was supposed to be a charming smile.

"Just a bit of it," Byron said with a shrug. "As it happens, Edmund, you two actually seem quite happy together. I could hardly believe what I was seeing, first outside and then at dinner. I thought for sure that you would be miserable. There is no question that I was certain she would be back to London already. Have you placed some kind of spell over her to hold her here?"

Edmund snorted. "It must be my good looks and charm."

Byron eyed him with so much contempt that Edmund was taken aback.

"I was always jealous of you, you know."

"Of me?" Edmund's head reeled. His brother had never said such a thing before.

"You never had any of the expectations placed upon you that I did. And still, you were good looking, silent, but with this mysterious air about you that the women seemed to enjoy, though why, I shall never know. Then when you signed up, oh, you were a soldier on top of it all! Father was so proud of you. He would often lament the fact that I was the one who would inherit."

Edmund could only stare at Byron in shock. "I never knew that."

"No, he made sure you never did. Wouldn't want to show too much pride in us, you know. He had no qualms in sharing his thoughts with *me*, however."

Edmund rubbed his forehead. He pitied his brother, but he didn't see how any of this was his fault.

"Look, Byron—"

"And then you came back from war." Byron's eyes took on a mysterious gleam. "You were a war hero, sure, but you were no longer a glorious, good-looking war hero. You were injured. Damaged. So scarred that people could hardly look upon you. And you hid away, here at Hollingswood, and suddenly I was favored again. I was betrothed to a woman with a dowry enough to pay off our family's debts and fund my own lifestyle. All was finally going well for me. Then our parents insist you attend my betrothal party, and suddenly she's yours, as is her dowry. To do what with? Update this decrepit estate?"

Edmund stared in disbelief. "You have no one to blame but yourself." He rose, unable to stomach his brother's inane accusations any longer. "Go home, Byron. You have a wedding of your own to prepare for, and there is no reason for you to extend your stay here."

"So that's it, then?" Byron stood himself and turned around. "You're not going to help me?"

"There's nothing I can do for you any longer," Edmund said, shaking his head. "Not until you learn to help yourself. Go get married, settle down, have yourself a couple of children. Leave Hannah and me alone."

Byron's face turned downright nasty then as he spat venomously at him. "You will rue this decision, Edmund. Mark my words." He marched over to the door and wrenched it open. "I'll be gone in the morning."

When the door slammed, the painting of his great-uncle Andrew rattled ominously behind him.

"I know," Edmund said to it as he sat heavily in the chair. "Thank goodness."

12

Hannah had sensed Edmund's discontent when he had come to her bed last night. It was late, and he hadn't made love to her, but instead tossed and turned. He hadn't left her, though, and she knew it was because of Byron's presence in the house. He was protecting her, for which she was grateful.

By breakfast, Byron had departed, and they had both breathed a sigh of relief. Hannah could tell that Edmund was still agitated, though he wouldn't tell her why. Instead, he spoke of his ancestor once more.

"I feel as though I'm to do something for him," he said with a sigh. "I just don't know what."

"If only he could tell you," Hannah said half-jokingly, although she wasn't entirely sure she would want a spirit speaking to her. The fact he was within the house seemed to be enough. "What are you doing today?"

"There's a fence that needs fixing," Edmund said, pushing food around his plate, though Hannah noticed he wasn't actually eating anything. "Thought I'd go see to it."

She could tell that what he really needed was some time alone, so she didn't comment.

"You?" he finally asked gruffly.

"I think I'll paint," she said, to which he gave a distracted nod.

A short time later, she and Molly were set up behind the house, but Hannah couldn't keep her gaze from straying toward the ruin.

"This is wrong," she said to Molly, who looked at her quizzically. Hannah was thinking on Edmund's words that morning, and she couldn't say why, but she felt that's where they should be. "We need to go to the ruins."

"Oh, my lady..." Molly said, her face falling. "Are... are you sure? I know it's not my place to say, but there's something about that place that is ever so frightening."

Hannah thought for a moment before gathering up her canvas and paints, placing them in the basket beside her. "I don't need the easel," she said. "I'll go alone. You stay here."

"No, my lady, I should—"

"It's fine," Hannah said with a reassuring smile. "It's not far and I don't have much to carry. Besides, there is no one about and I will not actually go into the ruins. I will simply sit outside."

"If you're sure..." Molly said, seeming torn, but Hannah placed a hand on her arm and nodded.

"Very sure."

"All right, then," Molly said before scampering back to the house, as though she was trying to leave before Hannah changed her mind.

Hannah noted the gloomy day as she began to make her way to the ruin site. She would have to keep a close eye on the clouds and ensure that if they became any darker or any closer, she would return. She had no wish to be caught in the rain with her canvas, for it would be difficult to find more. It was not as though the village nearby would carry any – what she had, she had brought with her.

When she finally reached her destination, she looked around, spotting a large outcropping of rock where she could set up and begin to paint. Only... she found it wasn't the view beyond that called to her, but rather the ruins themselves.

Hannah wasn't sure how long she sat there, mesmerized by what was before her. The wind whistled through the trees nearby and the old guesthouse seemed as though it was trying to tell her something, but she couldn't quite understand just what it was.

"Are you there, Isabel?" she asked, somehow not feeling entirely foolish to be speaking with a spirit. Leaving the canvas under a rock on the ground before her, she took a few steps toward the ruin, wrapping her arms around herself as she stared into it, the wind, now blowing briskly, chilling her through.

"What do you need?" she murmured. "You and Andrew... how can we bring you back together?"

She was so focused on what was before her that she didn't hear anything else until the click of a pistol hammer sounded just behind her ear.

"Hello there, little one."

Hannah screamed as she tried to whirl around, but his arm came fast and tight around her waist, holding her securely against him. She tried to squirm out of his grip, but it was no use – he held her fast.

"Let me go!" she shouted, trying to stamp down on his foot, but he only laughed sinisterly in her ear.

"What are you doing out here alone?" Byron asked, and Hannah recoiled from his breath upon her neck.

"Don't you know better but to be accompanied wherever you go?"

"What do you want?" she asked, breathing deeply as she tried to rid herself of the panic that had overtaken her. "Why are you doing this?"

The cold steel of the gun came to her temple, and as much as she attempted to hold it in, a whimper escaped her.

"I came here to Hollingswood with the expectation that you and my brother would be as miserable as I am," he said, his voice bitter. "It's what he deserves, after all. Then, much to my surprise, I find the two of you happily playing house together. I could have forgiven it, had he only made amends by providing me what I was due – a good portion of your dowry. But alas, my selfish brother turned me away at that. He told me to leave, in fact. So," he continued airily, "I am only doing what is necessary, in order to even the scales."

"Are you going to k-kill me?" she managed.

"Yes," he said, as though pleased with her for understanding his motives, "then he can be as miserable as I will be."

"I'm sure Edmund will reconsider giving you the dowry," she managed, despite the quivering of her lip, which she willed to slow in order to not provide him with any satisfaction, nor fodder to use against them. "I'm sure he had no idea what was at stake."

"I've decided I no longer care," he sneered. "If I must be miserable, then so will he."

Despite the fear quaking through her, Hannah's heart dropped at her brother-in-law's words.

"That's so sad," she lamented, "stealing someone else's happiness will bring you no joy."

"Perhaps not," he returned, "but it may bring me some satisfaction, which is the next best thing."

"Byron!"

Hannah nearly cried at the sound of Edmund's voice ringing through the air – just as the first drop of rain hit her square on the nose with a sting from the force of the wind upon which it fell.

Byron chuckled in her ear as he turned her around to face Edmund.

"Brother! I am so glad you have joined us. This will make it all the better. I had planned for you to find your lovely bride's body here among the ruins, but to have you watch her demise... well, that will be just positively delightful."

Edmund's face was so full of torment that Hannah forgot her own fears, suddenly overcome anew by the need to survive, if only to prevent her husband from having to suffer through watching another death.

"You are mad," Edmund said with disgust, and Hannah could feel Byron shrugging behind her.

"Not mad. Simply bitter. Bitter that no matter how things seem to be going wrong for you, you rise up and are made well again."

"You do know that you could have had it all," Edmund said, maintaining his even temper despite the wild panic in his eyes. "You still could. Let Hannah go and then return home. Make the best out of your marriage. It is possible – I know firsthand," he said with a look over toward Hannah. "You have no suffering, no scarring. You can be a good man, Byron."

"He may not bear scars," Hannah finally spoke up, willing her husband to understand that he had nothing to be ashamed of, that there was far worse than the battle wounds he wore on his face and his heart. "But inwardly, his soul is black, Edmund. You have seen and you have felt the worst pain, but it has only caused you to be a different man, a better man. Byron clearly feels nothing at all."

Byron dug the barrel of the gun into her temple at her words, and Hannah cringed. Edmund stepped forward as though to stop him, but Byron must have warned him back with a gesture, for he stopped short.

"Rethink this, Byron," Edmund pleaded. "We may never have been close, but this is no way for brothers to treat one another."

"It's too late for that," Byron said.

With a look of resignation, Edmund reached behind his back and quickly pulled a pistol from his waistband.

Hannah's heart began to beat faster with the hope of rescue, but Byron was quick to put a stop to it.

"You'll never shoot," he said with a laugh, pulling Hannah tighter toward him. "There is too great a chance you could miss and hit your beloved bride. Oh, how poetic that would be, if *you* were the one to kill her!"

Edmund said nothing as he lifted the pistol, pulled back the hammer, cocked the gun and looked down its barrel. Hannah trembled for a moment at the steel that covered his eyes as he stared down his brother.

"Let. Her. Go."

"Don't shoot him, Edmund," she said as she blinked away moisture from her eyes, unsure if it was her own tears obscuring her vision or the rain that was pouring in earnest from the sky now. "I won't let you have another life on your conscience. I couldn't bear it."

"Listen to your wife, *brother*," Byron snarled. "Now say goodbye."

Hannah's heart seemed to leap out of her chest, and when she heard the sound of a gunshot, she squeezed her eyes and let out a scream. She stood there, braced, waiting for whatever was to come next. In an instant, she found herself free of Byron's grip, and all she heard was silence. Was this perhaps Heaven? Had she not felt anything because she had died upon the bullet's impact? That was a blessing, at least, she thought, as she finally garnered the courage to open her eyes.

Only to find Edmund rushing up to her, wrapping his arms around her and crushing her hard in his embrace.

"HANNAH, OH HANNAH," Edmund kept murmuring in her ear as he held her close and stroked her hair, her back, her arms, never, however, letting her go.

He didn't think he ever would again.

"Wh-what happened?" she muttered, pushing back slightly away from him, but he held her face into his chest.

"Byron is... going to need some medical attention."

Now she really pushed away from him and he finally relented, though he regretted it a few moments later when he felt her intake of breath as she stared down beside them in horror.

"Did you shoot him?"

"No," Edmund said with the surprise he had initially felt as he gathered her back up in his arms. "He was so worried about hiding himself behind you so I wouldn't kill him that he left his entire arm out to the side. I was about to shoot his gun hand, even though it would have put you at risk, but then he must have taken a step back or unsettled something, for an entire chunk of what used to be the roof came tumbling down upon him. He seems to be knocked out, though I must say I haven't checked overly hard to see if he is still breathing as I don't really care. My God, Hannah, are you all right?"

"I am, yes," she said, looking up at him, resting her chin upon his chest. "Thank you, Edmund."

"If it wasn't for me, this would never have happened."

"Don't say that," she said, and he nearly lost himself in the depths of her eyes, wondering whatever he had done to deserve such a woman.

Suddenly his gaze moved from her to beyond. There, hung as though it had been set there days and not years before, was a picture of a woman staring back at him – one that seemed quite familiar.

"Hannah?" he said quietly, turning her around, though he kept her in his arms, "I think I know what we are supposed to do."

"You mean with Byron? What—oh." She finally saw the painting. "She's beautiful."

"She has a likeness to you."

"Perhaps," Hannah said, tilting her head, "though many differences as well."

Edmund wrapped an arm around her shoulders as they walked toward it. He released her only long enough to lift the painting off the half wall and tuck it into the crook of his arm.

"I think we best return this to the house."

"I think that Isabel would like that – as would Andrew," she said, smiling up at him. "Now come, we should go find Falton to help you with Byron."

"We should," he said with a sigh, and, with her leaning on him, they made their way back to the house, ignoring Byron's cries behind them.

EPILOGUE

Hannah curled up in the crook of Edmund's arm, the two of them sitting on the sofa in his library. She sighed contentedly as she nuzzled up into him.

"Are you all right?" he asked for what she thought must be the thousandth time that day.

"Yes, Edmund," she said with a slight laugh. "I do wish you would stop asking me. The better question, I think, is if *you* are all right."

"I don't think I will ever be all right again," he said with a sigh, and she leaned her head back against him.

"You thought that before," she said, "and things were getting better, weren't they?"

"Yes," he finally said slowly, "although perhaps that was wrong. It was as though things were becoming *too* good, and they had to give somehow."

"But Edmund," she insisted, "everything turned out fine. Byron is returning to London as we speak, being carefully watched by Falton. And you know if there was ever a man you could trust, it would be he."

"I know," he said, a self-conscious smile curling his lips as his voice caught.

"And," she continued, "we were able to determine what it was that Andrew and Isabel needed – each other." Hannah turned around, looking at where they had hung her portrait next to his. "I think they will be happy now, don't you?"

"You better be, you wily old fox," he called out, wondering if his great-uncle was even present anymore to hear him.

"I think," Hannah said slowly, "that they can rest in peace now, for they have one another and can be content in knowing that their story has been revealed. While *our* story," she looked up at him with a smile, "will continue on."

"I cannot believe how close I came to losing you," he muttered.

"But you didn't," she said, lifting her hands to the sides of his face – both the scarred and the unmarred. "Isabel saved us. And the threat is gone now. Byron will be returned to London, and will be watched over to ensure that he can never hurt another."

She went quiet for a moment. Then, "It is probably for the best this happened, actually."

Edmund nearly came off the sofa. "How can you say that?"

"Well, can you imagine what he would have done to his wife, had he married, or his children? At least now we know that others will remain safe."

"You are far too good, Hannah," he said, looking down at her, his eyes filled with unshed tears.

She looked up at him with a smile. "I love you, Edmund," she said, "and I always will."

He pressed his lips against hers, and for a moment she wondered if she would ever hear the words from him.

"I love you too," he said, and she didn't think her heart had ever been so full.

"Do you really think you can live here, with me and only me, out in the middle of nowhere?"

"We are not in the middle of nowhere," she argued. "There is a village nearby, full of wonderful people. And we will have to hire at least another servant or two, especially once we have children."

She smiled at the thought of it – until she looked at his expression.

"What's wrong?"

"Do you think... they... our children... will be frightened of me?"

"Of course not," she said with as much determination as she could muster. "How could they be? For you will show them the same love and protection you show me. And they will love you as much as I do."

"Someday... when my father passes, I will likely have to see to the other estates if Byron is declared mad. But I'll find good men to oversee them and will do all I can to remain here. Do you have no desire to return to London?"

Hannah thought it over, remembering the city, the people, the smells...

"Not at all," she said, shaking her head. "Perhaps a visit to my parents now and again, but we can always go see them when they are home for the summer months instead. I am happy out here, Edmund. I love this house. I love the spirits within it. I love the forests that surround it. And most of all – I love you."

"I'm not always the most companionable of people."

"Perhaps not," she said with a laugh. "But after all you

have been through... you still have such capacity for love, Edmund, which is more important than anything else."

"Only because of you," he said, looking down at her with such affection that her heart seemed like it was reaching out of her body toward him.

"Because we found each other," she said with a smile.

Behind Edmund's shoulder, Hannah noticed a candle flicker, as though someone had walked by it. When she looked over at the portraits, she could have sworn she saw their expressions change to smiles. She nudged Edmund, nodding toward the portraits.

He looked at them for a moment before returning his gaze to her, and then the air in the room changed and suddenly Hannah just knew that, finally, they were alone.

Edmund looked down at her, his lips lifting at the corners. "All is right," he said, and Hannah nodded at him in return.

"It's as it should be," she said. "Always your love."

"And always yours."

Then their lips found one another in a searing passion – a promise of all they had been through and all that was to come.

EXTENDED EPILOGUE

Hannah Marshville cherished these moments.

Moments alone. Moments with those she loved the most. Moments away from the world, in this intriguing house, with this beautiful family she and Edmund had created.

She took a deep, satisfied breath, opening her eyes as she took her paintbrush in her hand and leaned back into the cushions of the sofa. She swirled the orange and yellow paints together to create the perfect hue as she tried to capture the fire, the flickering of the flames that her son was currently so enraptured with.

"Careful, Simon!" she couldn't help but call out, causing Edmund to look back at her with a smile that was lovingly understanding and Hannah couldn't help but shrug. The worry never rested – even if her husband was holding both children in his arms.

Her four-year-old followed his father's gaze and turned to grin cheekily at her, a look which she returned. It was hard not to smile at Simon, who seemed to understand that there was no match for his charm.

She had sketched and painted her husband and children enough times to fill an entire art gallery, and still, she could always paint more.

It was hard to believe this was her life, that she and Edmund had found such happiness in a home that, at one time, had been filled with such misery.

"Mama?"

"Yes, darling?" she said, putting down her paintbrush and accepting that she likely would not have the opportunity to paint much longer while the children were still awake. And that was just fine.

"Can I paint?"

"Of course, Katie," she said, flipping over the page to a new sheet of canvas and moving out of the way for her daughter to paint instead. Edmund and Simon began a game of dominoes on the floor, and Hannah sat back and took in the blissful scene in front of her.

Simon laughed at something Edmund said and she smiled. Edmund had been so worried that his children would be afraid of him, or ashamed of him, but the opposite couldn't be truer. Unlike the relationships between parents and children that Hannah had grown up with in society, she and Edmund had created a real home here, a real family, and she wouldn't trade it for anything.

Her smile fell as her stomach flipped over, and she stood abruptly enough to catch Edmund's attention and concerned stare.

"Hannah? Is everything all—"

She didn't have time to listen to him finish his sentence, however, for she was already running down the hall as fast as she could.

"Hannah?"

Edmund pushed open the door of their bedchamber after he finished putting Simon and Katie to bed. His niggling worry about his wife wouldn't leave him, but he knew not to push Hannah. She would tell him what she needed to in her own time.

"Yes?"

She whirled around from her place at the vanity, putting down the brush, and he was arrested by the sight of her long, golden-brown locks. He walked over and took the brush from her, turning her around as he pulled up a chair behind her and pulled her back into the vee of his thighs.

He ran the brush through her hair, and she sighed as she closed her eyes and leaned back into his touch. He knew how much she loved the feeling of another brushing her hair, but the truth was, he took just as much pleasure from it as she did.

When her tangles were gone and her hair was shining in the flicker of the candlelight beside her, he wrapped his arms around her and drew her close, nuzzling his face into her neck.

He inhaled, breathing in the lavender scent that always accompanied her.

"Now that the kids are in bed..."

"Yes?" she opened her beautiful, wide brown eyes and met his in the mirror.

He smiled, knowing what she was expecting, but he surprised her.

"Would you like to go for a walk?"

"A walk?" she asked, startled, and he nodded into her shoulder.

"A walk. We'll ask Mrs. Ackerman to listen for the children, just in case."

"Sure," she said with a nod. "A walk would be lovely."

They found their cloaks and headed out, through the grounds that were now a flourishing landscape and into the night sky, the moon shining the path in front of them as they walked, unspoken, toward the ruins beyond.

Edmund wrapped his arm around her, pulling her in close, and he leaned her head into the crook of his shoulder, just where she belonged.

She sighed, and he looked down at her, kissing her head. "Is everything all right?"

"Of course it is," she said. "It couldn't be better." She tilted her head up toward him. "Why did you want to walk?"

"I had some news to share, and I wasn't sure when would be the right time."

"Oh?"

"With Byron's growing madness, my father has been having some trouble overseeing everything. He has asked that I come to London for a few weeks now and again, to help him with things."

Hannah nodded slowly. "We knew this day would come."

"We did," Edmund said. "I cannot truthfully say that I relish the thought of returning, but at the same time, I'm not sure what else to do."

"Well, I suppose we go and spend some time there, see our families, and in the meantime, you start hiring the people that you know can best help look after everything. We can return now and again as needed."

He squeezed her in tighter. "One of the very many reasons that I love you," he said, "is your ability to make everything seem so simple."

She laughed lightly, looking over the old ruins that stretched out in front of them.

"Do you think we should be rid of these?" she asked, gesturing toward them. "I'm worried sometimes, that the children will get into here and hurt themselves."

Edmund eyed them, understanding what she was saying.

"I agree with you, although I must say that it somehow seems... wrong to take them away."

"I know."

"I'll speak to Felton. Perhaps we can clean them up without actually being rid of them. Take away some of the pieces that could fall, remove debris from the ground."

"That sounds perfect."

She turned in his arms, and he wrapped them around her back.

"How did I get so lucky as to be with you?"

"I'm the lucky one," he said, his heart swelling to the extent that he wondered how it remained in his chest – although the truth was, part of it was out here, walking around in front of him. "To have you, and Simon and Katie, it's more than I ever would have dreamed for myself. Who ever thought, that Byron's tryst with that young woman – who, I am told, did find herself a respectable enough husband, if not as titled as they would have hoped – would have led to such happiness for us? I always knew my life would be here, at Hollingswood, but was convinced it would be alone. Except for Felton, of course."

"Of course," she said with a laugh but then sobered. "I have some news myself. You are going to have to make a bit more room in your heart."

"For Felton? He is already there, although please don't ever actually tell him that."

"No," she shook her head, lifting her eyes to his. "For another little one."

"Another..." his eyes widened and his heart seemed to stop for a moment. "Truly?"

He leaned back and placed his hands over her flat stomach.

"Yes," she exclaimed, laughing at his shocked expression. "Truly."

He picked her up, twirling her around before setting her down and thoroughly kissing her, pouring all his love for her into the kiss that he never wanted to end.

Finally he had to pull away, only so that he could lead her back to the house.

"Edmund."

She tugged on his arm, and he stopped with her, following her finger, which was pointing up to the sky.

"Look," she breathed, and he blinked, not trusting what was in front of him.

"It couldn't be," he shook his head.

"But it is," she insisted, laughing out loud with incredulity. "Two shooting stars. Oh, Edmund, I can't help but believe that it is Andrew and Isobel, looking down on us. I think we've done them proud."

"You couldn't do anything but," he said with a smile. "I love you, Hannah."

"And I love you, Edmund."

"Always."

"Always."

THE END

～

Dear reader,

I hope you enjoyed reading Hannah and Edmund's story! I wrote this book for an anthology, not thinking I would enjoy writing a Gothic romance. I was so wrong! I found this one fun and refreshing to write, and loved that Hollingswood Manor became a character on its own.

If you enjoyed this book, you will love Designs on a Duke, which also features architecture as a main part of the story! You can read an excerpt in the pages after this one, or go right to download it here: <u>Designs on a Duke</u>.

If you haven't yet signed up for my newsletter, I would love to have you join us! You will receive Unmasking a Duke for free, as well as links to giveaways, sales, new releases, and stories about my coffee addiction, my struggle to keep my plants alive, and how much trouble one loveable wolf-lookalike dog can get into.

<u>www.elliestclair.com/ellies-newsletter</u>

Or you can join my Facebook group, Ellie St. Clair's Ever Afters, and stay in touch daily.

Until next time, happy reading!

With love,
Ellie

~

Designs on a Duke
The Bluestocking Scandals Book 1

HER SECRET WILL SAVE A LEGACY. **But it could also break her heart when faced with a duke caught between two identities.**

The daughter of a famed architect, Rebecca Lambert has been raised among the nobility yet understands the circumstances of her birth. Becoming an architect is a dream, not an option, until she must assume an identity to protect her father's name.

No one was pleased when Valentine St. Vincent was shockingly named the Duke of Wyndham -- least of all Valentine himself. He has always led with his fists, but now he must become the man his brother was supposed to be.

When Valentine hires Rebecca's father, she takes on the work herself. But as she spends more and more time at the duke's homes, she finds herself hopelessly falling for a man she can never have. For the Duke of Wyndham must marry a woman for her dowry and respectability -- two things Rebecca can never provide.

Will Rebecca and Val resign themselves to the lives chosen for them, or those they were born to live?

AN EXCERPT FROM DESIGNS ON A DUKE

Valentine St. Vincent, the sixth Duke of Wyndham, was tired.

He was tired of balls. He was tired of operas. He was tired of pretending to be the Duke of Wyndham when all he had ever aspired to be was a man making a name for himself in his chosen profession, which was the only thing he truly excelled at. One who would be perfectly happy spending his life without any pressure or great responsibility placed upon him.

But then his brother had died. His father had died. His cousin was deemed illegitimate. And then the old duke had finally succumbed to the illness that had kept him bedridden for years, and Val remained the fortuitous one to be alive and declared the duke after a lengthy inquiry by the College of Arms.

He let himself into his house — though it was styled more of a mansion than anything else, and finding his butler utterly absent, he hung his hat up himself.

A crash resounded from down the hall and he smiled to himself. Jemima. At least some things never changed. His sister was still as curious in unraveling the next great scientific discovery. He didn't understand half of it, though she was always more than pleased to provide a running commentary of her most recent hypothesis. Currently, it was something to do with the effects of the cleanliness — or lack thereof — of water.

He strode through the foyer to what was supposed to be a ballroom but had become Jemima's laboratory. He found her blonde head bent over a microscope, so focused that she didn't even look up when he walked into the room.

"Good to see you haven't destroyed our new home quite yet," he said, and she yelped as she jumped up.

"Val! You scared me."

He chuckled as he tapped a hand against his leg, where an old injury still aggravated him from time to time.

"Where is everyone?"

"Hmm?"

Her mind was still elsewhere.

"Dexter wasn't at the door. Usually he is so eager to prove himself as a new butler that I can hardly untie my own cloak."

"Dexter? Oh yes, he came through here not long ago."

"Jem?" He tried not to sigh in exasperation, but he only needed a moment of her time.

"Right. Ummm, he had some people with him. I think they went into the parlor. So did Mother."

She waved her hand toward the end of the room, where the parlor was located.

"People? Oh, right — the architect." He slapped a hand to his forehead. "I completely forgot."

"And you call me absentminded."

When she finally looked up at him, her eyes widened and she snorted.

"You certainly cannot greet them looking like that."

"Why not?"

"You look as though someone just gave you a sound pummeling."

"I actually came out the victor, thank you very much."

He looked down at himself and saw that his sister had a point.

She was shaking her head now.

"I really don't understand why you continue to go back to Jackson's."

He walked over to the table and tweaked her nose as though she was still a girl and not a woman over twenty.

"And I don't understand why you enjoy mixing your liquids in here all day, but I leave you be, don't I?"

"Fair point."

"Very well. I best wash up and then I'll meet with the architect. Though I wish Mother hadn't pressured me into hiring one. We have no money to pay for him."

"That's why you're supposed to marry someone wealthy," Jemima said absently, returning to her work, apparently dismissing him.

Val sighed as he found the stairs and began to trudge up to his room. Truth be told, the only joy he could find in his current life was through some physical activity and boxing served the dual purpose of keeping up his strength as well as releasing the tension that seemed to build as he sat at his damned desk all day working in the ledgers the old duke had left. Val had fired his man of business who had supposedly handled everything but truly bungled it all. Val was determined to figure this out on his own before he trusted another to look after things for him.

He entered the large ducal suite, aware that it was too depressing, too dismal. It made him feel as though he was living in some remote Scottish castle. He'd have the architect take a look at this room, see if there was anything to be done.

Although his sister had said that *architects* had arrived — he only recalled asking one to come to consult with him. He certainly couldn't afford two. Hopefully the man had simply brought an assistant.

He stripped off his bloody shirt and threw it on the bed, realizing as he did so that he had forgotten to call for the valet, and Dexter wouldn't know to tell Archie he had returned. Well, soon enough, word would get round that he was home and Archie would be through the bedroom door and ready to offer him his assistance as well as his commentary.

He was not the most conventional of servants, but he was one of the few not constantly awaiting his every command, which was beginning to unnerve him.

Well, until Archie arrived, he supposed he could select his own clothes.

He opened the door to his dressing room, reaching out a hand as he did — and touched something very soft, very silky, and very smooth.

"Who's there?" he demanded, opening the door wider to allow more light in.

There stood a woman, her greenish-brown eyes wide as they stared at him over a pert nose. Her jet black hair was pulled back from her head, seemingly long and straight as pieces tumbled down from the pins over her back. What he couldn't tear his eyes away from? Those cherry-red lips, just begging to be kissed. They parted now, as though she was about to say something, but just then he heard a sound from the corridor.

"Your grace?"

Not Archie. Dexter.

For a moment, Val forgot that he was a duke, that he had no one to answer to but himself. He went back to being a young man, who was frightened of his father discovering any transgression. Before he could even think of what he was doing, he stepped into the dressing room, nearly pressing himself against the woman, and shut the door behind him.

~

REBECCA STOOD SO STILL in shock that she had no idea what she was supposed to do next. She was an intelligent woman. She should have a witty response on the tip of her tongue.

But inspiration had never come quickly to her. Rather, she had to stew on something, turn it over in her mind until just the right thought entered and answered her current problem.

"Ah... you must be the Duke of Wyndham," she finally managed before sensing movement. "Did you just nod?"

"I did," he said, his voice deeper, rougher than she had expected. "My apologies. Rather idiotic of me. Yes, I am the Duke of Wyndham."

"Well, I cannot say this is how I thought I would make your acquaintance."

"Rather silly for us to be hiding in here," he said with the slightest of chuckles. "I, ah, saw a beautiful woman, heard a voice in the hall, and acted on instinct."

"To hide with a woman?" she asked, pleased that he couldn't see the flush in her cheeks at being called beautiful.

"Err..."

"You don't need to answer that," she said quickly. What had gotten into her?

But then he laughed. His laugh was a low rumble that began deep in his chest before resounding throughout the dressing chamber. It was one of those laughs that was so contagious, one had no choice but to join in.

And so she did. It was freeing, chasing away both the awkwardness for a moment and the need for either of them to say anything within this strange encounter.

"I think he's gone now," the duke said after their laughter subsided, and sure enough, the sounds of his butler calling out "Your grace?" was no longer. "Poor Dexter. He will be most distressed. At least he likely found my shirt to take to the valet for laundering. That should keep him busy for a time."

"Your shirt?"

"Yes, it had some... stains."

"I see."

Rebecca was quite confused by this entire encounter, but who was she to question a duke?

"I, ah, best be going now," she said, slowly inching around him, doing all she could to not slide her body over his as she sought the door. Relief swept over her when she found the handle, and she turned the knob open, allowing light to enter once more though she didn't look back. "I shall see you in the parlor," she managed, before slipping out the door and nearly running out of the bedroom, along the corridor, and down the stairs.

VALENTINE STOOD THERE IN SHOCK, staring after the beauty. One look at her and he had turned into a blithering fool.

It was this entire new situation, he told himself. He was having a difficult time learning how he was supposed to interact with his peers, his servants, and... whoever this woman was. As she had escaped his room so quickly that he nearly wondered if she had seen a mouse, he realized that he had no idea who she was or what she was doing in his bedchamber. Apparently not a gift, he realized with a rueful laugh.

He was right in that his soiled shirt had been taken away, but he knew it would take him a great deal longer to dress himself than with the help of his valet. With company about he was expected, as a duke, to always be fully dressed in a waistcoat and cravat, as uncomfortable as they were. He walked to the door, throwing it open.

"Archie!" he bellowed, but instead of seeing his valet approach, a tall, distinguished gentleman he had never seen before was wandering down his corridor. What in the...

"Hello, sir," the man said, "to what do I owe the pleasure?"

"Ah... I'm not entirely sure," Val said, scratching his hair, which had been cut fairly short upon his arrival in London. He missed his usual longer locks. "Just who are you?"

"Why, I am Albert Lambert, of course."

"Lambert — the architect. Right," Val said, frowning. What kind of architect had he hired? "I thought you were awaiting me in the parlor."

"The parlor? We finished the parlor weeks ago!" Lambert said, further confusing Val. "We must now continue with the ballroom."

"That will be the last of it," Val said. "We must make sure we build my sister a proper laboratory first."

"Laboratory?" the man repeated back to him, a frown marring his face. "I wasn't told of a laboratory."

"Yes, well, I will explain everything when we discuss the project further," Val said, relieved when he saw Archie approaching down the hall. "I will be down to meet with you shortly, Mr. Lambert. My apologies for my tardiness."

He stepped back into the room, Archie following him with a questioning look, as Mr. Lambert nodded and strode away in the other direction.

My, but this was a strange day.

∽

KEEP READING Designs on a Duke here!

ALSO BY ELLIE ST. CLAIR

Reckless Rogues
The Earls's Secret
The Viscount's Code
The Scholar's Key
The Lord's Compass
Prequel, The Duke's Treasure, available in:
I Like Big Dukes and I Cannot Lie

The Remingtons of the Regency
The Mystery of the Debonair Duke
The Secret of the Dashing Detective
The Clue of the Brilliant Bastard
The Quest of the Reclusive Rogue

The Unconventional Ladies
Lady of Mystery
Lady of Fortune
Lady of Providence
Lady of Charade

The Unconventional Ladies Box Set

To the Time of the Highlanders
A Time to Wed
A Time to Love

A Time to Dream

Thieves of Desire

The Art of Stealing a Duke's Heart

A Jewel for the Taking

A Prize Worth Fighting For

Gambling for the Lost Lord's Love

Romance of a Robbery

Thieves of Desire Box Set

The Bluestocking Scandals

<u>Designs on a Duke</u>

<u>Inventing the Viscount</u>

<u>Discovering the Baron</u>

<u>The Valet Experiment</u>

<u>Writing the Rake</u>

<u>Risking the Detective</u>

<u>A Noble Excavation</u>

<u>A Gentleman of Mystery</u>

The Bluestocking Scandals Box Set: Books 1-4

The Bluestocking Scandals Box Set: Books 5-8

Blooming Brides

A Duke for Daisy

A Marquess for Marigold

An Earl for Iris

A Viscount for Violet

The Blooming Brides Box Set: Books 1-4

Happily Ever After

The Duke She Wished For

Someday Her Duke Will Come

Once Upon a Duke's Dream

He's a Duke, But I Love Him

Loved by the Viscount

Because the Earl Loved Me

Happily Ever After Box Set Books 1-3

Happily Ever After Box Set Books 4-6

The Victorian Highlanders

Duncan's Christmas - (prequel)

<u>Callum's Vow</u>

<u>Finlay's Duty</u>

<u>Adam's Call</u>

<u>Roderick's Purpose</u>

<u>Peggy's Love</u>

<u>The Victorian Highlanders Box Set Books 1-5</u>

Searching Hearts

Duke of Christmas (prequel)

Quest of Honor

Clue of Affection

Hearts of Trust

Hope of Romance

Promise of Redemption

Searching Hearts Box Set (Books 1-5)

Standalones

Always Your Love

The Stormswept Stowaway

A Touch of Temptation

Unmasking a Duke

Christmas Books

A Match Made at Christmas

A Match Made in Winter

Christmastide with His Countess

Her Christmas Wish

Merry Misrule

Duke of Christmas

Duncan's Christmas

For a full list of all of Ellie's books, please see
www.elliestclair.com/books.

ABOUT THE AUTHOR

 Ellie has always loved reading, writing, and history. For many years she has written short stories, non-fiction, and has worked on her true love and passion -- romance novels.

In every era there is the chance for romance, and Ellie enjoys exploring many different time periods, cultures, and geographic locations. No matter when or where, love can always prevail. She has a particular soft spot for the bad boys of history, and loves a strong heroine in her stories.

Ellie and her husband love nothing more than spending time at home with their two sons and Husky cross. Ellie can typically be found at the lake in the summer, pushing the stroller all year round, and, of course, with her computer in her lap or a book in hand.

She also loves corresponding with readers, so be sure to contact her!

www.elliestclair.com
ellie@elliestclair.com

Printed in Great Britain
by Amazon

47269451R00078